DANCING WITH A SHADOW

MONSTERS OF THE REALMS:
BOOK 1
QUELL T. FOX

CONTENT WARNING

Dancing With a Shadow is a Paranormal Monster Reverse Harem novel.

It is the first book in a series and ends on a minor cliffhanger.

In this book you will find

- Murder

- Explicit sexual scenes

- Cheating (not in the harem)

- Mention of history of sexual assault of a minor

- MM scenes

Introduction

It is said shadow men lurk in the shadows, watching and waiting. These mysterious beings exist in a realm which parallels our own, hidden from human eyes. Born of darkness and bound by an age-old pact, they are the silent guardians of humanity—and more.

When malevolent forces threaten the fragile balance between light and darkness, the shadow men step into the light. Cloaked in inky shadows, their eyes gleam like twin orbs of moonlight. They move with an eerie grace, their footsteps unheard, their presence felt only as a shiver down one's spine, ready to eliminate a threat.

But beware, for these guardians do not only protect, they also bear witness to the darkest depths of human souls. They know the secrets whispered in the dark and the sins hidden beneath *the mask of day. To invoke their wrath is to invite shadows to consume one's very existence. For other creatures linger in the shadows too—blood thirsty and mindless.*

So, the next time you feel a chill down your spine as you walk through an unlit street or glimpse a fleeting shadow in your peripheral vision, remember the shadow men. They are there, silent watchers in the Realm of Shadows, safeguarding the world from the true horrors that lie just beyond the edge of the night.

Chapter One

LEXIA

My legs refuse to move. There isn't a single part of me that wants to be here, yet I can't get my body to work so I can leave. Even my eyes won't shut when all I want to do is close them. I don't want to see what I'm seeing, but I can't turn away.

Maybe it's not what it looks like.

Don't be an idiot, Lexia. Your contacts may be coming up on expiration, but you aren't blind. It's exactly what it looks like.

But why?

Why is he doing this?

Why does my boyfriend have his lips all over Cassie? Why are his hands on her hips, holding her ass against his dick as they dance?

No, not just dance.

Grind.

Why are they together when he is supposed to be here with me?

Sure, he didn't expect me to be here. I said I wasn't coming to prom because I didn't feel well—and that *was* true. But I woke up this morning and felt better, so I decided to surprise him.

Well, it seems I'm the one who's getting a surprise.

A shitty surprise.

My chest tightens as his hands slide further up, resting just under her full breasts. She smiles, laying her head on his shoulder. I want to throw up.

There they are, just thirty feet from me, dancing like lovers.

He grabs her hand and spins her, then tugs her against him again.

He smiles down at her with stars in his eyes—no, not stars. *Hearts.*

Does he love her?

He says he loves me.

But he doesn't look at me like that.

I grit my teeth and whirl around—a little too quickly, it seems. I must be lightheaded from what I've seen because I lose my balance just enough to bump into someone walking by.

They shout, "What the hell!" Then cold liquid covers my chest. I groan, glancing down at the red punch splattered all over the bodice of my white dress. *It's ruined.* There is no way this is coming out.

4

Mom spent so much money on it. She picked up a lot of overtime to afford this dress. Now it's ruined. And I didn't even get to dance in it.

All I wanted to do was dance.

"Watch where the hell you're going, dumbass!" someone shouts. Maybe the person who spilled their drink on me. Maybe someone else.

"Sorry," I mutter, and take one last glance over my shoulder at Bradyn, which is a mistake.

He meets my eyes, and his widen, but he doesn't move away from Cassie. We stare at each other for a long moment before I pull my gaze away and leave the gymnasium. My heels click on the floor as I hurry down the hall to the exit.

I need air.

"Lexia!" Bradyn calls out, but I keep going. I can't let him talk me into staying here. I know what I saw. Three years with the most popular boy in school didn't make sense from day one, so it certainly doesn't now. Which is why him grinding all over Cassie, the head cheerleader, makes sense. It's why, even if I hadn't seen it with my own eyes, I'd believe it.

They belong together.

Football star. Cheerleader.

That's logical.

I'm just Lexia Keissenger. The smartest girl in school. The nerd. The one no one wants to be friends with. The poor one. The freak. The nutcase. And whatever else they call me. I'm not the girl Bradyn James dates. Yet... I was.

It only makes sense it would end like this.

I burst through the double doors, sucking in a breath when the warm night air hits my skin. I hurry to the steps, lifting my tulle skirt so I don't trip on it, and make my way down the cement stairs.

"Lexia, stop!"

"No!" I scream over my shoulder and keep going.

I make it to the bottom, feeling eyes on me. There are students everywhere—chatting and talking, making plans to skip the prom and go somewhere else. Laughing. At me, no doubt. They all knew. They must have. I'm the school joke. How long has this been going on?

Bradyn catches up to me right before I hit the grass. He grips my upper arm and pulls me to a stop. I whirl toward him, hating that I'm crying.

When did I start crying?

"That wasn't what it looked like," he says, his chest heaving.

"Don't lie to me, Bradyn!" I shout, tugging my arm free and stepping away.

"I'm not, it—"

"Yes, you are. Don't act like that was nothing because it *was* something. A big something. I was watching for..." I wipe my eyes, trying to hold back the tears. "For way too long."

Bradyn searches my eyes, and I take in his brown ones. I used to love looking into them. If I hadn't seen the way he was looking at Cassie, I still may. They used to be so kind, so sweet. Lately, they've been nothing but shadowed. Like he's hiding something. Now I know what it is.

He sighs, running a hand through his hair. "Okay, you're right," he admits. "But she doesn't mean anything to me."

"No? Then why?" I ask, my voice breaking. "Why do it?"

A group of students gathered at the top steps watches the drama. Bet everyone will know about this scene I'm making before the night is through, and I'll be even more of a freak show when I get to school on Monday. Thankfully, there's less than two weeks before graduation. I won't have to deal with them for much longer. I've handled it all this long, I can deal with two more weeks.

"I don't know," he murmurs, stepping closer. "I just... I'm confused."

"Well, I hope this clears things up for you. We're done." Turning on my heel, I hurry through the parking lot. I only cry harder when I don't hear his footsteps coming after me. The urge to look over my shoulder is heavy—maybe I just can't hear him and I'm being dramatic. I won't give him the satisfaction, so I keep going.

My heels sink into the damp grass at the edge of the lot. A trail through the trees cuts out onto my street. I'll be home in ten minutes if I go this way. Otherwise, it'll take me at least forty-five to go around. I'm not calling my mom to pick me up, because that's embarrassing as hell. At least she won't be home when I get there, since she's out with her friend for a drink tonight. I'm grateful for it. I can go home and cry myself to sleep without her asking what's wrong.

I don't want to talk about it.

The trail through the trees is dimly lit by fairy lights so the students can walk through safely. It looks magical, but it doesn't feel that way. It should be beautiful, but I feel nothing but pain. No, I don't even feel pain, just empty. Why has every man in my life disappointed me?

I slow down halfway through the trail. It isn't long, maybe three school buses in length, but I'm running out of steam. The adrenaline is wearing off, and all I want to do is fall into a heap on the ground.

All I wanted to do was dance.

There aren't many people who know about my love for dancing. It's not something I make known, because it's just more fuel for everyone to use against me. But Bradyn knew. He knew how upset I was I had to miss prom because I was sick. He told me he was upset too. Said it really sucked that we were missing our senior prom together. Doesn't seem like it sucked for him at all.

I huff out a laugh and shake my head, coming out of the trail and onto the sidewalk. I walk the curvy road but stop a few houses from mine when my mother's car is in the driveway. *Shit.* She said she was going out. Why is she home? I can't face her like this. Not with the way I look and definitely not with how I feel. I look around and spot Park Street a short distance behind me. So aptly named, as the street ends at Hailemont Park. Guess I'll spend my prom night on the swings, all by myself. At least they won't ask me questions.

CHAPTER TWO

VESPERON

I step into the darkness of the crossover, letting it cover me, walking until the air shifts to something less heavy. I follow it until I reach the moonlight, stepping out into the trees of the human world. The cool air hits my being, and I breathe in greedily. Another beautiful night on patrol.

Over five hundred years of this and I am still as proud as ever to be a Guardian of the Realms. It is a prestigious position not all Shadows are trusted with. Guardians have an important job to keep the realms safe from the evil that lies within the Shadow World—one of the darkest and most dangerous of all the realms. As a guardian, I make sure those horrid creatures stay where they belong—in the darkness. In my five hundred years, I have only had to stop two entities from crossing over. Guardians are the last point of protection, but the most vital, as we are the last protector of the next realm.

Plenty of dark beings—or darklings as they are commonly referred to as—linger around, hiding in the shadows, lying low in wait for the perfect opportunity to escape and wreak havoc upon unsuspecting victims. They enjoy blood. Similar to demons, they kill, rape, maim. They are the worst of the worst. Those who have attempted or succeeded in causing harm to another being are banished to the prisons. Some escape.

I like to think I am good at what I do. The area I protect is relatively quiet compared to the larger cities. Hailemont is small, quaint, and calm. It requires only seven of us to watch over. Due to it being less active, some creatures assume it will be an easy entrance. I have never let one pass me, though. Not in all the years I have been doing this has a creature gotten past me and into this realm. The guardians in the big cities have smaller areas to watch over and are sometimes constantly at battle, but I am happy with what I do, regardless. I do not need to be in the throes of action every day to feel proud.

Being a guardian is a solitary job. We give up friendships and freedoms and even our mates—but it is a fair price for a lifetime of glory. There is nothing in this realm or another that I would give my title up for. I am loyal to my duty, and that will never change. Some Shadows are born with the need to feel pride, while others need to feel power. Though we originate from the same place, not all are designed the same.

I walk back and forth, sticking to the shadows as I patrol. This part of my section is the most quiet—the park. I am not required to stay hidden in the shadows, but I have more power this way. The darkness gives me energy which I will need if I have to fight off a creature trying to come through. Being in the light, even the moonlight, for long periods of time drains my energy. I am a creature of the dark, even if my habits do not seem so.

Luckily, the many times I have been spotted, the humans have been clueless. They assume it is their mind playing tricks on them or a trick of the light. Some Shadow Guardians enjoy scaring the humans in jest, but I do not. Perhaps this is why the humans think everything lurking in the shadows is out to get them. Little do they know how many of us are actually here to protect them—to keep the balance of light and dark.

Before my days as a Guardian of the Realms, I was a Guardian of the Castle. When we are born, we go through extensive testing to see what our life's duty will be. There are many duties for shadows, not only guarding. Some reproduce, others rule. There are travelers who explore the realms and return information to those who figure out which realms need more protection than others.

There are many arguments over which is the most important and satisfying, but my vote is for this. Guardians of the Realms. We are in the front lines, in a territory that is not necessarily safe and not entirely friendly. Being here for long periods of time makes us weak, especially those who patrol during the day. I am grateful my duties are during the night. By the end of a shift, I am exhausted. I cannot imagine how the day guardians feel.

The night is quiet. I have not felt anyone walking around. Nothing outside of the mess of the school. There must be another dance going on, or perhaps a sports game running late.

As a Shadow, we sense emotions, even from long distances. So, even though I cannot see my entire area, I feel when anyone enters it.

I prefer to stay at the park because it tends to get a lot of activity from adolescents who think it is fun to play with Ouija boards and perform séances. Many think they are destined for magic and do all sorts of wild things. And even though they may not have the ability to call upon something properly, just the presence of a Ouija board attracts the dark creatures. They lie in wait, hoping the silly kids will do something correctly and actually call upon them. It rarely happens. Still, messing with them is against my advice, as you never know what you will summon.

I cannot stop anyone from doing these sorts of things, or anything, really, as I cannot interact with the humans, but if they were to succeed, it is then my duty to step in and bring the dark creature back to the Shadow Realm.

It is not always easy to ignore the humans, especially those with big emotions. I am closely related to demons and feed off negative energy. It, like the dark, gives me strength. But as a guardian, we are taught to ignore attraction to emotions that tend to excite us. It is different for everyone, but I am extremely attracted to sadness. Most feed from hate or anger.

This is why being a guardian takes a strong being. It is not for the weak. All it takes is one weak guardian to allow creatures to pass from the darkness, and the human world would be overtaken. It has happened before, many times, and causes absolute chaos. Wars, serial killers, school shootings... some of the most horrific things were caused by rogue shadows allowing the darklings through.

For any of our worlds to exist, there must be balance. I understand that, as do the other successful guardians, but the evil beings lurking in the dark do not. All they care about is feeding themselves with hatred and causing chaos and destruction.

Time passes slowly, as it normally does, but I must always be on guard. If I allow my walls down for even a moment, it could be detrimental to both our worlds.

I linger beneath the trees and stare up at the moon. It is not full, but almost. It is a beautiful sight, something we do not have in the Shadow Realm which is made up of darkness. If it were not for us being home to other creatures too, like witches and fae who help with certain duties, we would live in complete darkness. But because of these creatures who need light to see, we have artificial lighting made by our kind, which does not take our energy.

I pull my gaze away from the moon when I feel an abrupt spike in emotion. A heavy sadness moves toward me quickly from the east. It is strong. Stronger than I have felt in a long time. My instincts kick in, and I want to run to it, take it all, feed from it. I close my eyes and take a breath, steeling myself before I check it out.

Remember your duty, Vesperon.

When I have collected myself, I move deeper into the trees and to the east. Someone is here and they are unhappy. It is alluring, such a strong and thick feeling. I have never been so tempted to take something in my life. This is... alarming. There must be a group of people. There is no way all this sadness belongs to one person. I stop when the emotion almost consumes me.

I suck in a deep breath and smell the sweetest scent. Vanilla. Cinnamon. Scents we do not have in the Shadow Realm, but I have learned of them from the humans. It is so calming, so...

I look around, confused over what I am sensing.

One person.

How can this be one person?

Humans have a lot of emotions, and tend to be dramatic, but they do not usually feel so deeply.

The emotions grow around me, and I dig through them.

Sadness. Embarrassment. Shame. Betrayal. Hurt. Anger.

There are so many. So many lovely feelings...

I must see who the owner of such beautiful things is.

I step closer to the pathway that moves through the park and regret it instantly.

The girl walking toward me takes my breath away. She is the most gorgeous being I have ever set eyes on, and her feelings are so profound. There is an ache in my chest. An ache so fierce I am sure it will be branded there forever.

This girl calls to me in a way she should not. As a guardian, I am not capable of having a mate.

Yet... I move from the safety of the shadows and trees, risking everything.

14

CHAPTER THREE

LEXIA

The park feels empty, which I am grateful for. The kids who normally hang out here are likely at the prom, or maybe they've moved on to the after party at Jonah Tomlin's house. He's the rich kid in school—the son of a big-shot lawyer in one of the big cities an hour away. Why they live here is beyond me. I swear it's because they want to show off. Sure, here they're the big cheese, but in a city? They'd be mediocre at best.

My stomach rolls when I think of how I was supposed to go to that party with Bradyn.

I still can't believe what I saw—what he did. How could he do this to me?

Three years... Three whole years of my life wasted. All for nothing.

How long has this been going on? How many people knew and didn't tell me?

I'm such a fool. *I am such a fool!*

I'm an idiot for thinking things would last with Bradyn. He told me he loved me, said it all the time. Said he would love me forever... but it was all bullshit. I should have known better.

I stop at the end of the walkway and pull off my shoes, dropping them right there in the dirt, then make my way across the damp grass to the swings. I don't care that my dress will get dirtier—it's already ruined. What's some mud on the bottom of it when the top is stained with bright red punch?

I reach the swings and sit down, then I kick my feet off the ground to give myself a push. The breeze rustles my hair but feels good on my face. I close my eyes and let the swaying relax me. It takes a few moments, but the ache in my chest lessens. My tears dry up. I can breathe easier. My thoughts don't stop, but at least I'm thinking more clearly.

How am I going to show my face at school on Monday? What's the difference? Everyone probably already knew. Finding out isn't making me any more of a fool. In fact, it's the not knowing that does.

Part of me wants to go back to the school right now and find some guy to dance all over. Make out with. Go to the after party with. But it'll never happen—not in this school. No one likes me. They only tolerate me because Bradyn was dating me, but now? I doubt anyone will ever talk to me again. Not that I even care. I'm fine being alone. As long as they don't go back to bullying me, I should be fine. Hell, even if they do, it won't be a big deal. There isn't much time left.

Bradyn and I never made sense anyway.

The jock doesn't date the nerd. The fact we'd known each other since we were little kids shouldn't have matter. Actually, I guess it didn't matter. It made no difference in how we ended up.

"Lexia, you really are an idiot," I mutter.

"Lexia..."

The voice of someone saying my name breezes past me like a whisper. I glance around, trying to see who it came from.

"Hello?" I call out. It was probably the wind and my mind playing tricks on me. It's windy tonight and there are a lot of trees around. A lot of whistles and whooshes through the leaves and branches.

I kick my feet on the ground and give myself another push. I close my eyes and lean back, straightening my arms and holding my weight. My hair flows around me, and I feel like I'm flying. Smiling to myself, I open my eyes to stare up at the moon. A waxing gibbous. Science has always been my favorite class, especially when we talk about the stars and planets and everything else up in the sky. I bet no one up there would bully me. Sometimes I wish I would get abducted by aliens. Taken to another planet and made their queen, like in those fictional romance books.

A girl can dream.

I sit up, resting my head against the chain and let out a sigh.

"So beautiful..."

I jerk my head to the left, certain I heard something that time. It wasn't the wind.

"Who's there?" I call out, putting my feet down and standing up. "Hello?"

A chill runs down my spine even though it's warm. There isn't much crime in our town, but it's still a possibility. It's probably kids from school who've made their way over and want to give me a hard time. I roll my eyes and move back toward the walkway. I should get home anyway.

I pick up my shoes but don't put them on. After a few steps, I hear that breathy voice again.

"Do not go..."

I stop and look over my shoulder, my heart rate picking up.

"You're not funny!" I call out. I scan the area, and swear I see something move in the woods. "Bradyn, is that you? This is really stupid," I say. "You need to stop."

I stare for a long moment, then move closer, ready to call him on his crap. But I don't see anything.

"Bradyn?" My voice comes out weaker this time, and I'm officially freaked out.

"Beautiful..."

The voice comes again, and chills erupt across my body. That doesn't sound like Bradyn or anyone else I know. It doesn't sound human.

"He-hello?" I call again, still staring into the woods. Something moves, something that looks like a person. I don't know if that makes me feel better or worse. I move a little closer. "Who's there?" I ask.

Something in the shadows moves again, and I see a figure. A tall, dark figure moving toward me.

I step back. "D-do I know you?"

"You do not..."

The figure moves closer to me, and when it reaches the edge of the woods, almost in the moonlight, I see it fully. I gasp and step back. Every part of my brain is telling me to run, but I don't. I can't.

What I'm looking at is not human. It's like a ghost. Like a human made of only shadows. Though the sight shocks me, I don't feel frightened. Adrenaline courses through me, but it isn't fear.

"I will not hurt you," it says, this time its voice is more solid. It sounds human now. Deep, raspy but with a slight echo to it.

"What are you?" I ask.

"I am a shadow," it answers.

I'm grateful it stays put.

"A shadow?"

"A Guardian of the Realms."

I take a small step back. The thought that I'm talking to a demon crosses my mind. There's a whole group of kids who like messing around with dark magic stuff, but I'm not one of them. Anything outside of this world should be left alone. If it were meant for this world, then it would be here.

Yet...

"What does that mean?" I ask.

"Why are you not afraid?" it asks, tilting it's head to the side.

I keep my eyes on the figure. It's shaped like a human. Has all the human features, but more prominently with darker shades of whatever transparent substance it's made from. It's tall and thin. It's barely darker in color than where it's standing, making it difficult to see. If I stare for too long, it blends in well. When it speaks, its mouth moves but just barely. It's like he is there but not at the same time.

"I am," I say.

"I feel your emotions, and fear is not one of them."

"You do?"

"It is what drew me to you. Your sadness and shame... it is so sweet."

Sweet? How are those emotions *sweet*? I look around again, realizing how ridiculous this is. It has to be a joke. Like a projection or something. This can't be real. The kids from school are probably recording this, wanting to make me out to be more of a freak than they already think I am.

"Thanks for that... I guess. Well, it was nice chatting, but I have to go." I turn to leave.

"Do not leave," it mutters, almost sounding disappointed. Sad.

"Sorry, but it's late," I call over my shoulder, my heart still pounding as my feet move slowly.

"Return to me," it says, moving along the tree line in the same direction I am going. My gaze darts to where the trees end, just a short distance. I pick up speed. What if this thing *is* real? What if it's a demon that wants to possess me? Or eat my heart?

"Yeah, okay. Sure. When?" I say, trying to appease it but continuing to walk.

"Tomorrow night."

The end of the trees is a short distance now.

"Sure. See you tomorrow," I say, then jog, gripping my shoes in one hand while lifting my skirt with the other. I run until I reach the end of the park, then I turn and swear I see it standing where the trees end—watching me.

My heart is pounding, but still... I don't feel fear.

CHAPTER FOUR

VESPERON

My shift ends when the sun peeks over the trees. I walk deep into the woods, away from the park, and stop at the point where the darkness feels like home. Just as I reach it, Averial comes through. Humans cannot get through the crossover, which is why the entrances are not more hidden. Humans pass them often and don't know any different. They feel nothing.

"Slow night?" Averial asks. He is a strong shadow, both physically and mentally. Though we can take any shape, as shadows are amorphous, we go with what is most comfortable to us. It is why we do not all look the same. Some shadows are taller than others, some more muscled.

"Thankfully," I respond.

He nods. "Sleep well," he tells me, then walks off.

Guardians work in shifts constantly. This is my life. There are no days off, no vacations, no breaks. There is the time I am working and the time I am not, which is when I sleep to regain my strength for another patrol.

I step farther into the darkness, and I allow it to pull me back to my realm. Once there, my body takes on its solid shape. Here, I am real. I start the walk to the Guardian Castle—the castle which is home to all the guardians in this area.

As I walk, I spot the prison off in the distance. Its peaks jut into the sky like knives, and the screams of the darklings echo all the way over here. At one time, I wanted to work there, to keep the darklings within its spelled walls, but when the time came to choose, I went with guarding the realms instead.

Our realm is made up of many zones, and you stay in the zone according to your duty. Female shadows are not allowed in the guardian zone, as they are not allowed to be guardians. Their skills are better utilized in other areas. Women do not have as much choice in what they do as male shadows.

The walk to the castle is not long, but it feels like it is taking forever.

I cannot get that girl out of my head. This is concerning.

Lexia... what an interesting name. Humans have such strange things, and their names are an example of that. But it is not her name that is pulling my attention from all that is around me. It is everything else. Not only her innocent face, bright eyes, full lips, and curvy body, but the way she felt things. The emotions rolling through her, stronger than I have ever felt from a single human. It was overwhelming. Harder to ignore than ever before.

"Good morning, Vesperon." I look up, realizing I have reached the castle. Zenba, one of the gatekeepers, is standing there with a smirk.

"Good morning, Zenba."

"How was your shift?" he asks.

"Well. Quiet."

"Wish I could say the same."

"Ah, it was a fun night, then?" I ask with a knowing smile.

"Drunkards and a loose darkling."

"Makes for good stories," I answer.

He chuckles, and I continue through the gate and up the stone pathway to the castle doors.

Though we are not allowed friendships, we socialize.

From spending so much time on earth, I hear the things people say about creatures of the night, but they are not true. Well, *that* is not exactly true. There is some truth to what is said. Some creatures of the night want nothing more than to cause you harm. But there are others, like me, who do not want harm to come upon anyone. I do not quite wish them to be happy either. Those like me, we just exist. Like a balance, I suppose. Not all of us are good. Some are the scary things in the night that haunt houses and possess people and steal souls. Shadows, like people, are born good and bad.

I nod at the doorman, Zhotelm, who pulls open the tall black wooden door for me, and I enter. There are countless castles in our realm, housing our kind. We do not have single dwellings like humans and other species.

Not only do we guard the limits in the human world, but we guard them in other worlds too. Because of this, shadows are knowledgeable in the way many beings live.

I take the stairs because my mind will not stop. My energy has been depleted more than usual over speaking to that girl. We are not supposed to do such things, and pushing ourselves when we are not corporeal takes more out of us than if we were. Had I fed from her energy, I would have been fine, but I will not allow myself to do that. It would take nothing from her, but for me... it could be catastrophic. One taste and I may never stop. Yet even though I feel so tired, I also feel restless.

I walk up five flights of steps to reach my floor. The castle goes up and down and has thousands of rooms to house the guardians. The castle is grand. So grand I have never seen the whole thing and I have lived here for as long as I can remember—many millennia.

I walk down the main hallway and make my way to my room in the north end. I pass many rooms with open doors, the occupants sleeping, reading, or lounging. Many close their doors, but none of them lock. If you can be trusted to guard, then you can be trusted to not go into a room that does not belong to you. The Guardians of the Dark—the umbrella name for all guardians—are loyal and honest. And if they are not, then they are dealt with.

I step into my room and move to the aperture that overlooks the black volcanoes. I hear on earth they have volcanoes too, only they spew orange and red lava. Here, it is black and purple, and if you are lucky, you will see blue. They erupt often, and the sight is incredible.

I wonder what Lexia is doing. Has she fallen asleep yet? Has she thought of me?

I realize how wrong it is to continue thinking of her. A human. Why am I thinking of a human? I should not think of anyone, never mind a human. Guardians are not allowed attachments. We, like most creatures, have sexual needs. We may act on them, on our own or with others, if we choose. But they are to be left as an encounter and nothing more. Relationships are out of the question, no matter how casual they are.

A knock on the door has me turning toward it.

Jhaixl is stepping into my room with a smirk. He is a handsome shadow, one I am fond of. I have known him for many years.

"Thought I saw you walk by my room." I smirk back at him, then turn to the window. "Long shift?" he asks.

Jhai and I work the same shift but on opposite sides of town. I guess what we have could be considered friends with benefits, as the humans call it, but I would never call him that here. It is not allowed. But what we do for the other is just that. We take care of each other's sexual needs without question.

Guardians are not perfect, and over the years, plenty of them have gone rogue. Murder. Rape. All of it. Not only against other guardians, but the species we protect too. This job is not meant for everyone, and the process of weeding out the weak-minded is not perfect.

"It was," I admit.

He moves behind me, sliding his hand down my arm. I look at him over my shoulder and already know what he has planned. I am not opposed to it. Perhaps, this is the encounter I need to take my mind off that girl permanently.

Jhai's hand slides to my shoulder, then his other is there too. He massages the tension away, and after a moment, my mind calms.

"I know just the way to make you relax," he whispers as his hands glide down my back, all thoughts of the girl gone.

CHAPTER FIVE

LEXIA

Sometimes, I truly think I've lost my mind. I've always been different, I've accepted that. I enjoy school, don't like going out to parties, don't like staying out late. I love reading and going to bed early. But talking to monsters? This is on another level. If I thought I was stupid for trusting Bradyn, I'm even more of an idiot for doing this.

Most people run when they see shadow creatures. They get scared. They have a *normal reaction.* They don't stop and talk to them! Yet, what did I do? I stood there and talked to it! It followed me, told me not to leave, said I was beautiful, then asked me to go back tomorrow.

Absolutely not.

I said I would, but I can't. This is insane!

What if it's a demon who wants to suck my soul from my body? What if this horrible creature will eat my insides? What if it possesses me and makes me do monstrous things? No, I absolutely will not be going back there tomorrow. Or ever. I'm not sure I'll ever go to that park again after tonight.

When I make it home, I'm grateful to see the driveway empty. I guess Mom forgot something earlier, or maybe her friend needed more time. I let myself in through the back door with the hidden key we keep under the garden gnome that sits on the step. Once inside, I press my back against the door and blow out a long breath.

What an awful night.

After taking a moment to collect myself, I push off the door and head down the hall to my room where I get out of this dress and head straight for the shower. What will I tell Mom happened with the dress? Best I hide it for now and worry about it later. I'll talk to her about this giant mess one day, but not tonight. Probably not tomorrow either.

I wash my hair and body, scrub my face to get all the makeup off, then crank the heat up and stand under the spray until the water gets cool. Once I'm out, I put on a pair of shorts and my favorite T-shirt—a faded Guns N' Roses shirt that was my dad's—and crawl into bed.

How on earth did my mother ever move on after my father died? I guess I can't say she moved on, but how does she get by? Especially after the one and only traumatic relationship she had after him. My mother seemed to bounce back fairly quickly after my father died, but I know now it was just a front. She did what she needed to do because of me. Because even though she was no longer a wife, she was still a mother. Her first relationship after my father was four years after he passed, and that was... bad. Worse than bad. He's in jail for what he did to me when I was just ten. Hopefully he rots in there.

After seeing Bradyn tonight, I feel like my life is over. I'm hurt and embarrassed. I've never felt such agonizing pain before—not like this. I never thought Bradyn would cheat on me. I questioned why we were together so many times, even wondered if it was some sick joke. But I never expected to be cheated on. I thought maybe he'd just break up with me, but this... this is so much worse. I feel like dirt. Worthless.

I jump when my phone vibrates from the nightstand by my bed. Bradyn's face pops up on the screen, and I groan, then reach over and reject the call. Talking to him is not what I want to do. Now or ever. If I never see him again, it won't be a problem. I don't care what he has to say. I don't want to hear his excuses.

My phone starts up again, and this time, I shut it off. I can't have him tormenting me all night. This hurts too much already, and I don't need him adding to it. Once my phone is off, I roll over and try to sleep even though I don't feel tired. I only feel sad. Confused. Sick.

Soft tapping sounds on my window, and I roll my eyes. That has to be Bradyn. It isn't the first time she's snuck in through the window. Did I lock it? I can't remember...

That question is answered when it slides open. My heart leaps from my chest. What if it *isn't* Bradyn? What if it's a serial killer breaking in to murder me? What if it's that demon? I press my hands to the mattress, ready to get up and run out the door.

I stare at the window, but even in the dark, I can tell it's Bradyn. He's snuck in so many damn times it would be odd not to recognize him.

"Get out, Bradyn!" I hiss.

"Not until we talk," he says, standing up straight. He closes the window, then turns back to me and runs a hand through his messy brown hair before shrugging off his suit jacket and untucking his white dress shirt.

"I don't want to talk," I say, turning my face back to the pillow.

The bed dips as he takes a seat beside me, and his hand rests on my upper arm. I shrug it off and scoot away from him.

"Lex, please..."

I sit up, facing him. "Please, *what*? What exactly do you want from me, Bradyn? It's shitty of you to ask me to do anything for you after what you did to me."

"I know that," he admits.

His eyes are filled with sadness, and it almost makes me feel bad.

Almost.

No, Lexia. No. You will not feel bad for him!

"Then get out," I growl, crossing my arms over my chest.

He pulls his gaze from me and looks down at the floor.

"I'm sorry," he whispers.

He gets up and leaves through the door. A moment later, the front door opens and closes. I wait a few moments before getting up and hurrying out there to make sure it's locked. I grit my teeth and stare at the door for a long moment before I give in and move the curtain aside to peek out there. He's nowhere in sight.

Good. If he was, I may have done something stupid like ask him to come back.

Chapter Six

VESPERON

Jhai slides his hand around to my stomach and presses his firm chest against my back. His erection rests against my ass, teasing me.

I have never had sex with anything other than a shadow, but I hear in terms of fun, we are top notch. Apparently, some creatures do not have control over their sexual organs, and whatever they are born with is what they have. They cannot make it bigger, thicker, longer... they cannot make it into two to fill both holes of a female at the same time. They cannot choose if they want it to be smooth or ribbed.

That is not true for Shadows. Being amorphous means we can transform our body into any shape we want, whenever we want.

"Do you want to lie down?" Jhai asks, dragging his fingers along my abs.

"Let us stay here," I say, allowing my eyes to fall closed.

"Grab onto the windowsill."

I lean forward and press my hands to the windowsill to hold myself steady and look out the window.

He uses his foot to spread my legs apart, then grasps my hips. Something hard gently prods at my rear hole, the hole that is there only for pleasure, as we do not need it for anything else. We do not eat, therefore we do not excrete waste. Not all shadows have these holes, as some choose not to give into their sexual needs needs—but most do. This is the most enjoyment we get.

"Relax, Ves," Jhai whispers.

"I am."

"I am already leaking for you," he says.

He presses into me with one appendage, the one he creates just for me. He is slick already, as he said. Shadows have copious amounts of reproduction fluid, which comes in handy as our pleasure holes do not self-lubricate. Not even the females.

Jhai easily slides into me, knowing I prefer when he is not too thick, but instead when he goes deep. He shifts his organ into what I like the most, while he pleasures himself with the other. There are many fun things to do when you can control what shape your sexual organ can take.

He fucks me slowly, almost lazily, in a teasing sense. I let him do this until the need to touch myself is too great to ignore, then I elongate my appendage and slide between my legs to find his entrance. I slip inside him as he reaches around to take me into his hand. The pleasure is so good. Tripled from Jhai in me, stroking me, and my tip in him.

I hear shadows enjoy orgies, splitting their pleasure organs into as many as their body will allow. I have never done such a thing but am not against the idea. For now, I am fine with it being just Jhai and me. Perhaps one day I will get more adventurous.

The volcanoes in the distance rumble, and I smile. Jhai moves faster in every way he can. The stress of the night falls away from me, and all I feel is pleasure. All I think about is Jhai and how I am so desperately ready to release my load, but he is not giving me enough.

"You are learning," he whispers in my ear. "You'll be rewarded for that."

I smile wider, my fingers digging into the stone of the sill. My eyes threaten to fall closed, but I keep them open, watching the volcanoes that will surely have an eruption tonight.

"I cannot finish like this," I say, frustrated.

"One day you will," he answers.

Maybe. Maybe not.

I need him to go faster, harder.

"I am so close," he tells me. I thicken the appendage in his hole, and he groans in my ear. The sound vibrates through me, and a wave of pleasure racks my body. I, too, am so close. "I want you to swallow it tonight," he says. "Give me your mouth."

I remove my appendage from him as he does the same. By the time I am facing him on my knees, his organ is back to only one. I watch in anticipation as he strokes himself faster, then look up at his face. As shadows, we can shape-shift, but we cannot change color. We are shadows, we are dark, and the only thing to make out facial features or to show off different body parts are the shades of our shadows. Darker and lighter shades of black.

Jhai grasps my chin and tugs me forward. I open my mouth for him. He presses the tip of his organ to my tongue, and with one last stroke, he is finishing. My mouth fills with his liquid, so much it spills out. I swallow it down, and he gives me more. It is sweet and warm, like nectar, and I thoroughly enjoy this. His orgasm lasts through three mouthfuls, and when I move my hand to wipe what has spilled from my chin, he grasps my wrist and tugs me up to lick it from me. When he is done, he drops to his knees and slides me into his mouth. I shift my organ to one that will fit better, and he sucks me hard, fingers digging into my thighs. The volcano continues to rumble outside. I let my head fall back on my shoulders as my stomach muscles tighten with release. It hits me out of nowhere, my knees shaking as I finish, filling up his mouth. He, too, gets three mouthfuls, and he does not waste a drop of it.

The volcano outside erupts, and I smile wide when the shadows can be heard cheering from outside and through the halls. It is almost as if they are cheering for me, but I know that is crazy.

Jhai hums in satisfaction as he gets to his feet, hands still on my hips. He spins me to face the window and we watch the last of the eruption together as we catch our breath.

When all is settled, he whispers, "Lie down." He guides me to the bed and lays down with me. We should not lie together like this. It is a grey area when it comes to our rules. Still, I cannot find it in me to tell him to go. Instead, I close my eyes, and sleep takes over quickly.

Soon enough I will be back at the park, wishing for Lexia to return, as she said she would.

CHAPTER SEVEN

LEXIA

I wake up before my alarm on Monday morning, and head to the shower while throwing my hair up so it doesn't get wet. I quickly wash up and get out. Mom is clanking around in the kitchen, probably preparing breakfast, so I hurry back to my room to change. The weather is warm, as it's almost summer, but I still put on jeans because I hate wearing shorts. I grab a plain black T-shirt, then put on my Keds and brush my hair into a ponytail before heading to the kitchen.

"Morning," I say.

Mom looks over her shoulder and gives me a tired smile. Her thick brown hair is on the top of her head in a messy bun and she's still in her blue floral night gown. So many people say we look alike, but outside of the dark hair and bright-blue eyes, I don't see it. Though, I don't see a resemblance to my father either.

"Morning, sweetie. I'm making eggs and toast."

"Sounds good." I go to the coffee pot and make myself a cup before taking it back to the table. When I sit down, Mom puts a plate in front of me full of eggs and two slices of buttered toast. A moment later, she comes to sit with me with her own plate.

"Are you excited for school to almost be done?" she asks.

"Definitely," I say as I stab a chunk of eggs.

"Have you gotten a dress for graduation yet?"

"I don't think I want to wear another dress, Mom."

"But it's your graduation," she complains.

"Yeah, and it's going to be under my gown, so no one will see it anyway," I argue.

She sighs, then says, "Fine. Whatever you're comfortable with."

"Thanks, Mom." I smile at her, and she shakes her head but smiles back.

"You still should get something new."

I groan. "I hate shopping."

"Come on, we can go together. I'm not working tomorrow. Let's go after school," she offers.

"Fine," I say, finishing my coffee. I take a few more bites of eggs, pick up my toast and bring my plate to the sink. "I have to get going before I'm late."

I hurry to my room with the toast in my hand, grab my backpack, and head back through the kitchen.

"Have a good day. I'll be home late tonight. I'm working second shift," Mom says as she gets up to bring her plate to the sink. As a nurse, she works all different shifts. She picks up whatever is available.

"See you later!" I call out as I head out the door.

As I pass by the street that leads to the park, a shiver runs up my spine.

Even though I told that shadow thing I'd go back on Saturday night, I didn't. What if it's evil and had plans to do something bad? I wonder what it wanted with me, but I'm not stupid enough to go back and find out.

I make my way down the street and through the woods to the school where kids are already hanging out in the grass and on the steps. People stare at me as I walk by, plenty of them smirking and attempting to hide laughs. Until I pass a group of girls who point and laugh without a care in the world. Whatever.

Entering the school, I am grateful the halls are mostly empty and go straight to my locker. When I open it, a stack of papers falls out, fluttering to the floor. I step back and reach down to pick them up. I must have thrown them in here last week in a rush. I left early Wednesday because I wasn't feeling well, and wasn't in on Thursday or Friday.

When I pick up the papers, I realize they aren't schoolwork I left behind. They're photos of Bradyn and Cassie. I look through them, though I wish I didn't. Some are of them dancing while others are of them making out... and not all of them are from prom on Friday. My stomach turns sour. Some of these were either taken over the weekend or before. I don't know which is worse.

When Bradyn left my house on Friday, did he go to her because I wouldn't forgive him? The nerve!

I crumple the papers, fighting back tears, and grab everything I'll need from my locker for the day. The mess mess of photos on the floor is someone else's problem. I hurry to my first period class even though I'm twenty minutes early.

Each period I celebrate a little because I've avoided Bradyn all day. I usually run into him between classes, but that was because he would seek me out. We have the same lunch, so there's no avoiding it now. Once I take a seat at the back table, away from just about everyone, I look around as I eat my turkey sandwich. I don't spot Bradyn anywhere, but I see Cassie and her gang of girls laughing and chatting away across the cafeteria. I've taken the last bite of my sandwich when Jordan, one of Bradyn's teammates and good friends, sits down beside me.

I raise a brow at him, not having the slightest clue what he could want. Though, it's possible he's here on behalf of Bradyn.

"What's up, Lexi?"

"It's Lexia," I comment as I reach for my water.

He holds his hands up in surrender, flashing me a grin. He is a good-looking guy, with bright-hazel eyes and light-brown hair. He's in shape, as are most the football players, but Jordan isn't just a football player, he's a *player* too. I think he's slept with more girls in this school than the rest of the football team combined.

"Sorry," he says playfully.

41

"What do you want?" I finish my water, then pile my trash on the tray, ready to get the hell out of here.

"Well, I heard you're single now and was hoping we could hook up."

What the hell?

I scoff. "Are you serious?"

"Of course," he says, winking at me. "You're one of the girls I never thought I'd get the chance to fuck, but... here we are."

My jaw drops open. "You're disgusting."

I grab my backpack and my tray, then get to my feet and hurry away.

"So is that a no?" he calls out after me. I shake my head and keep going.

I swear, these people are so dense!

I toss my trash and hurry out of the cafeteria, up to the library. It's where my next class is since I have a free period. I may as well get a start on my homework.

It takes a good half hour for me to calm down after the encounter with Jordan. What the hell is his problem? If he doesn't have some STD by now, I'd be surprised. I'd bet good money he's had at least two just this year. There's no way he's clean after sleeping with as many people as he has, and I've heard—though this could be a rumor—that he doesn't sleep with just girls. He sleeps with anyone willing. I don't have a problem with his, or anyone else's sexuality. My issue is with people being unsafe. And he expects me to sleep with him? He's out of his damn mind!

The only person I've ever slept with was Bradyn, and not often. We had sex for the first time at the beginning of the year, and we've done it maybe five times since. We've done other stuff more, like oral, and we've been doing that longer. It's what we're more comfortable with and what we enjoy doing.

Though, now that I think about it, maybe that's because he was sleeping with Cassie, and maybe Cassie doesn't like oral. Maybe she likes all the other stuff.

Oh my stars, I need to get checked! Even though we always used protection, you never know. What if she gave him something that he gave to me? Oh, could this get any worse?

My stomach twists, and I think I'm going to throw up. Shaking my head, I take a deep breath, then look back at my Chem book. I need to stop thinking about Bradyn, and Jordan, and any other guy, and focus on my work.

"There she is," someone hisses. I fight the urge to look up because I know whoever it is, is talking about me. It happens often. All this bad attention toward me isn't new. It happened long before Bradyn and I started dating, and even during.

When someone sits down across from me, I keep my eyes on my book. I don't want to deal with petty behavior. I just want them to leave me alone so I can finish studying for this test.

"Cassie sent me over here to tell you that she *wanted* to tell you what was going on between her and Bradyn, but she didn't want to upset you." I slowly look up, my hand tightening on my pencil, and meet Ashlynn's brown eyes. Not a single part of her feels bad. Her eyes are empty. Like most people in this school.

"Okay," I say, because what else am I supposed to say to that?

"She said Bradyn kept saying he was going to break up with you, and to keep it a secret because he would talk to you so you wouldn't freak out."

Why is she telling me this? It's obviously not to make me feel better... or does she think this will make me feel better? Is she that airheaded?

"Be sure to tell her I said thanks." I force the words out, then bring my attention back to the book, but the tears make the words blurry.

"They're better together anyway. Jocks shouldn't be with nerds like you. They should be with girls like Cassie."

I bite my cheek so I don't freak out. Thankfully, Ashlynn gets up and leaves. It takes a few moments, but I finally pull myself together and finish studying.

As I get through the last class of the day and make my way home, the only thing I can think of is how pathetic my life is now that Bradyn and I aren't together. Now, I really have no one.

Chapter Eight

VESPERON

It has been three nights since I saw my Lexia, and I have not stopped thinking about her. Her face has haunted my dreams, consumed my thoughts. I have considered going to look for her but instantly realized how foolish that was. Leave my post? What is wrong with me? It is possible no one would know, as I am not checked up on, but if something got through... how would I explain that? No, I need to stop thinking of this girl and get over whatever this is. No matter how much I think of her, it is clear she does not think of me, and it is obvious why. I am a monster. A shadow. A creature of the night that she, as a human, is taught to fear. Why did I ever think she would come back?

Why did she agree to?

It does not matter. She did not come back, and she never will. I need to stop thinking about her and focus on work, my duty. This job was my dream, and I will not mess it up. There could never be anything between us anyway. Guardians do not have mates. We do not have partners. We do not have relationships. The most we have is what Jhai and I have, which is purely sexual to relieve tension. Friends with benefits.

This sure feels like a mate bond though.

I would not know firsthand, but I have heard the pull is strong. That the thoughts of the person will drive you to insanity if you do not give in to it.

But I should not have a mate. I gave that up when I became a guardian. It is part of the swearing-in ceremony. The shadow witch strips the ability to have a mate from you. This is something all guardians go through, something we agree too. This is how it has been for thousands and thousands of years. How could it be that mine went wrong? It is unlikely.

Plenty of shadows may have their mates, as long as they are not guardians. There is a mate out there for all of us, some of us just choose to do something else with our existence, instead of being with someone.

What does having a mate give you? Nothing.

How does mating with someone enrich your life? Give you something to live for? They are only another person there with you, like a friend you have always.

Being a guardian gives my life meaning. It allows me to be proud of something.

A mate would not do that.

But then why have I considered doing things that could ruin my oath... and for a human?

I am confused. Perhaps I am getting a sickness. It has happened before, but not in a long time. Seven hundred years ago, or so. Though, I guess it is possible. I am not thinking clearly, and it would be a valid explanation.

I look up at the full moon, knowing I must be on guard tonight. Creatures always want to get out on the full moon more than any other time. I need to stop thinking about Lexia and worry about my duty.

I keep myself busy by walking back and forth through the trees and filling my head with the last time I was with Jhai. Thoughts of him occupy my mind and make the night go by faster. Perhaps when I return in the morning, he will want to have more fun. Maybe if I spend more time with him, this will all be easier. Perhaps I am just needing more attention lately. The full moon could be affecting me too.

Chattering fills my ears, and I duck deeper into the shadows so the humans do not see me. I am not myself if I am hearing them before I am feeling them. I need to pay better attention. I look out into the park and see two teenage boys walking through.

"—and she actually said no!"

"You're a fucking idiot, Jordan. Obviously she said no."

"What the hell do you mean?"

"She's not like the other girls. If you want to get in her pants, you need to be nice."

"I *was* nice."

"No, like really nice. You can't just go up to her and ask her if she wants to fuck you, you Neanderthal."

I roll my eyes. Even as a shadow I am not so stupid to think that would work. These children have much to learn.

The boys stop by the merry-go-round. One sits, while the other stays standing.

"I thought with her being such a nerd, she'd be into me. I'm Jordan Miller, bro. Everyone wants to sleep with me," the one sitting down says. He sounds like a fool.

"Well, obviously *she* doesn't."

"She will."

"Wanna make a bet?"

I move closer so I can get a better view. They are wearing sports jerseys, and I assume they go to the high school on the other side of the trees. I do not like gossip, but it is sometimes entertaining to watch how much the humans enjoy it. I have learned much about the humans and their way of living by watching. I have seen the way they grow and change. Hell, I remember when the school was being built. When there was no park here, only trees and the roads were only dirt.

"Oh, fuck yeah. What do I get when I win?" the one sitting asks.

"If you win, I'll convince my cousin to go out with you."

"The hot one with the big tits?"

"Yeah, moron. And if I win, you're giving me your jersey number next year."

"Fuck, bro... seriously?"

I smirk. Does he not think the terms are fair?

"You think you can get her to sleep with you, so what does it matter?"

"You're right. Fine. But be prepared to get your cousin well acquainted with me, because by the end of the summer, Lexia will be riding this dick."

Lexia...

His words echo in my head, and I see red.

CHAPTER NINE

LEXIA

"Sweetie, come here!" my mom calls from the living room. We just got back from shopping, and I'm in my room trying to sort through all the new summer clothes I got. We were only supposed to get an outfit for my graduation, but Mom really loves shopping.

I toss the shirt I was about to put on the hanger onto my bed and head into the living room. I find her on the couch, staring at the TV.

"What's wrong?" I ask.

She points to the TV. "Is this someone you know?"

I furrow my brows, moving deeper into the living room so I can see what she's talking about. Mom puts the volume up, and I realize it's our local news channel.

"—one in critical condition and the other dead. Authorities are asking anyone with information to come forward, and the families are offering a reward of 10,000 dollars to anyone who gives information that leads to an arrest. Authorities are going door-to-door to question neighbors to see if they heard anything. Here is Anita Houston with more on the story."

The screen changes to a woman standing in a park. The park right down the street. Behind her is crime scene tape and uniformed people walking around.

"I'm here at the scene of a devastating crime that's rocked Hailemont to its core. This town hasn't had a crime of this nature in over thirty years. Right behind me, you can see the crew searching for any evidence that could lead to who may have carried out this heinous act." She pauses, and two photos pop up on the top left of the screen. One of Jordan and one of his best friend, Scott, who also plays on the football team. My breath catches in my throat as I put everything together. "These two boys were out for a leisurely stroll last night around ten pm, and when they didn't return home, their parents started to worry."

"Turn it off," I whisper.

"Mindy Miller says sh—"

I take a moment to breathe, then turn toward my mother. "They're dead?"

She frowns. "One of them, sweetie. One is in critical condition."

"Which... which one?"

"I believe Jordan is the one who... I'm so sorry, Lex. Were you close with them?"

I shake my head as I sit down beside her. She puts her arm around my shoulder and pulls me close.

"No, not really. They were on the team with Bradyn, but we weren't friends. It's just... Mom, they were only seventeen."

She rests her cheek on my head. "The world is a scary place. Even in safe little towns like this."

We sit there until there is a knock at the door. We share a confused look, then get up together. No one randomly shows up at the house. I stay by the table as Mom walks to the door. She peeks through the curtain before unlocking and opening it.

"Good morning, ma'am. I'm Deputy Charmaine. My team and I are going door-to-door to see if they heard or saw anything suspicious last night."

"We didn't hear anything," my mother says, opening the door wider and stepping aside so the officer can see me. I shake my head, taking in his uniform and the gun on his belt. Guns have freaked me out since my father's death. The deputy's uniform is a dark blue, almost black, with an electric-blue stripe down the side. His hat looks like more of the cowboy variety and not officially part of the uniform.

The deputy nods, handing my mother a business card.

"This here is the tip line in case you remember anything or hear anything about what took place at the park last night. I assume you're aware of what happened?"

My mother nods. "Of course. I'm sure the whole town has by now. I'm so sorry for those boys and their families."

"I'll pass that along. Don't lose that now." He gestures to the card. "Even if it's something small, call and lets us know."

"We certainly will. Thank you, Deputy."

He tips his hat, turns and heads down the stairs. My mother closes and locks the door, then turns to me, her hand on her chest.

"I can't imagine what those families are going through," my mother chokes out.

She knows *exactly* how it feels.

She felt all that pain and heartache when my father took his own life. I felt it too, just differently. I was only six and didn't quite understand. Apparently, I found him, but I don't remember that part. Not consciously anyway. I have no problem remembering my fear of guns, considering that's how he did it. Subconsciously, I remember it all, I bet.

"I'm sure the person responsible will be found," I say, and my mother nods, a lost look in her eye as she stares straight ahead.

"I sure hope so," she whispers.

I think, sometimes, my mother doesn't believe my father killed himself. I think, sometimes, she thinks someone did it. Nothing ever pointed to that. It was clear what he did. The only thing making her think that is because it's too hard to accept my father would choose to end his own life and leave her and me, rather than get help.

I know it's not that easy of an explanation. I've read a lot on mental health. I did a project on it my sophomore year and dug deep because it hit close to home. Even though my mother is pretty laid back and "in with the times," there are plenty of things deep rooted in her because of the way she was raised. Showing her emotions openly is one of them. She tends to shut down. She doesn't want to admit my father chose to leave us or how much it hurts.

I think maybe he didn't choose it. It wasn't his fault he felt that way. He needed help; he didn't get it. Can he be held responsible for his actions because of that?

My father was dealing with something he couldn't overcome. He didn't know how to ask for help. So he did the only thing he thought would help. He made it all stop.

I glance out the window, in the general direction of the park, and all I can think is if I was the intended target.

CHAPTER TEN

VESPERON

"And you are sure you saw nothing?" Jlenar, my chief, asks.

"Yes, sir. I was at the far end of the park when it took place. I smelled the blood, and that is what drew me to them. By the time I got there, it was only the boys."

"And who was it that found them?"

"A man walking his dog. He frequents the park late at night. I have heard him speaking about being unable to sleep."

Jlenar nods, tapping his fingers on his desk as he walks around it. He stops in front of me, leans back, and keeps his gaze behind me.

His office is the most decorated room in the castle. As shadows, we do not have personal belongings, we do not keep sentimental things, all we have is what we need.

Jlenar's office has multiple bookshelves with many books, the most I have ever seen in one place, outside of the library at the school I have visited on occasion. He has a fine desk, made of the best dark wood in the realm, his chair matching. It is near black, but when light is upon it, it sparkles as if glitter is inside. It is a rare sight, considering most of us do not use lighting. There is a scroll hanging on the wall with the oath we all take as guardians, and then there is the plaque that names him as chief.

"This murder looks otherworldly," he murmurs.

"I assure you nothing got through to my zone."

He turns his gaze to me, stares at me for a long moment, then nods.

"I will be speaking with everyone in the area. You are free to go. If I have any further questions, I'll send someone for you."

"Thank you, sir." I get up from the chair, then head out of the room.

I walk confidently all the way back to my room, and even when I get there, I do not let my guard down. I can never let my guard down. Never again for the rest of my days.

I killed that boy. I tried to kill the other too.

And I do not regret it.

Those boys deserve what they got. How dare they speak about my Lexia that way? I made sure to tell them too. Made sure they knew exactly why their lives were ending. Am I concerned about the one still alive? A little. It is possible he will not remember or cannot explain what happened. But it is also possible he remembers everything, which is why I have to make sure he does not get the chance. But I have to be smart about this.

There are plenty of people in the shadow realm you can pay to get your dirty work done. That is not the issue. The issue is finding one without being caught. Especially now that I have already been questioned. Humans were harmed on my watch, in my area, and those in charge know it was not another human.

Guardians have no reason to go anywhere. Everything we need is within the castle walls. Therefore venturing out will only make me look guilty.

There is the possibility of doing it myself, but that is more difficult than it seems. Getting to the hospital will not be a problem, the problem is getting inside the hospital. They are always well lit, and I have no idea where I amm going. This will require some thinking.

"Everything okay?"

I look up to see Jhai standing in my doorway.

"I have just returned from speaking with Jlenar."

He gives me a knowing nod, then moves in to sit beside me.

"I'm scheduled to meet with him shortly."

"You? You are not even in the area."

"They're wanting to speak with everyone in the town."

"Or everyone who knows me," I mutter.

"Do they suspect you?" he asks, his brows furrowed.

"I am not sure." I fall onto my back on the bed. It is a small bed, but enough for me. I would like to share this bed with Lexia, this way she has to stay close. "It happened in my area, seems like they would."

57

"But you didn't see anything."

Yes... I did not see anything.

I spoke to Jhai about this when I returned. We are to report anything like this that happens, and I did that right away. The news spread quickly because nothing ever happens in the small town of Hailemont. Had I tried to cover it up, I would only have looked guilty.

"That is what I told him."

"Then I'm sure everything will be fine," he assures.

I consider asking him if he knows anyone who could help with this, but I cannot risk it. Jhai and I have an understanding with one another, and have for years, but he is still a Guardian of the Dark, meaning he is loyal to his duty, not to me. No matter how long we have been friendly. I can trust no one with this. I must do it on my own.

When I leave my room for my shift that night, I pay attention to my surroundings more than usual. I keep an eye on where everyone is, on how long it would take to walk to the darker parts of our world, to figure if I could do it without being caught. I realize that I barely see anyone once I leave the castle grounds. There is not much in our area. The problem is, that means I will not come across someone who can help me. Searching for someone is out of the question. I really will have to figure out how to do this myself.

CHAPTER ELEVEN

LEXIA

I lie in bed for hours, unable to sleep. My mind won't stop. I wonder if that demon had plans to kill me. That's what this was, right? Our town hasn't seen crime like this in a long time, now suddenly, there's a demon hanging out in the park and a teenager ends up dead.

I wasn't friends with Jordan, but I'm still sad he's gone. No one deserves to die like this. Not at such a young age.

My phone dings with a notification, and I roll toward it to see a text.

I sigh when I see it's Bradyn.

You up?

I stare at it for a long time before responding.

Unfortunately.

He doesn't answer me after two minutes, so I text him again because I feel bad. His friend just died.

Are you okay?

I don't know

I'm confused

Want me to call you?

I hate that I offer, but I can't help it. I'm angry with Bradyn for what he did, I'm feeling betrayed, but I still love him. He's still a human that needs someone right now.

My phone rings.

"Hey," I murmur.

"Hey."

"How are you?"

I already asked him that, but I don't know what else to say. Even on the phone, it feels weird with him. He's like a stranger, and I don't like it. He used to be my best friend. Now, everything is different.

"I don't know, Lex."

I hear the emotion in his voice, and it kills me. It strikes me right in the chest, and I feel like I can't breathe. I bite my lip and stare up at the ceiling.

"It's crazy that he's dead, you know? I don't think it's really sunk in yet," he admits.

"That's normal, Bradyn."

"I know that, I just... Everything is all fucked up right now."

"What do you mean?"

"If this had happened a few weeks ago, I'd be with you right now, holding you, and you'd make me feel better."

"Bradyn..." My bottom lip trembles as I listen to him.

"I'm sorry, Lex. I fucked up. I fucked up so bad, and I regret it. I had a lot of stuff on my mind, and it felt good for a while, but now, when things really matter, I realize that it was a mistake. I love you, Lexia. I love you so much, and I want to be with you."

"Bradyn—"

"Please, Lex," he chokes out. A tear slips from my eye. "I need you," he whispers.

"I'm here, Bradyn."

"But you're not mine."

"I know you're upset, but..." Another tear falls, and I wipe it away before continuing. "Maybe we should talk about this tomorrow, okay?" I can't talk about this right now. My head is all over the place. I know what I want to tell Bradyn. That it's too late. That I'll never look at him the same. He's ruined whatever could have been between us. But I don't want him to hurt more now than he's already hurting, so I decide to push it off. "Call me tomorrow, okay?"

He sighs, then says, "Yeah, okay. I'll call you tomorrow."

"Good night, Bradyn."

"I love you, Lex."

I don't know how to respond to that, so I just say, "I know," and end the call.

I drop the phone beside me on the bed and take a long, steadying breath before wiping my eyes again.

I can't forgive Bradyn for what he did. I just can't. Some people could, but that's not me. There is no way I'll ever forget what I saw. I'll never forget the way it made me feel. Maybe if I hadn't seen it, if I'd just been told or he admitted it, then it would be easier. But those images... they'll never leave my head. How will I ever be able to look him in the eyes again and not see him kissing Cassie?

Still, he needs me right now. And I can be there for him—as a friend. It won't be easy, but I can't be cruel. He made a mistake. Mistakes happen, I understand that, but he needs to understand I can't just forgive and forget like he wants me to.

But there is something I need to figure out, and I need to figure it out tonight.

The house is quiet as I tiptoe down the hallway. I slow as I pass my mom's room but pick up the pace once I hear her snoring softly. She rarely wakes up through the night, and I don't plan on being gone long.

Hopefully, she won't know I've left at all. She's always been okay with me going out, though the only person I ever went out with was Bradyn. I've never had a curfew or anything, but with a potential killer on the loose, she'd lose her mind.

I'm careful with the door, being as quiet as possible. The air is warm outside, the crickets chirping loudly. I hurry down the street, then turn the corner. My heart skips a beat when I see the park, but I keep going.

I need answers from this... creature. Whatever this thing is. I got away from it last time, so I should be able to do it again. I want to know if it was him who did it. And if so, why? I've never dabbled in any witchcraft or supernatural stuff. My family isn't overly religious. I think I have a fear over it from watching too many movies. But if this creature is here to cause my town harm, to hurt my friends, then I'll go all Sam and Dean on its ass.

I hold my head high as I step onto the walkway that leads into the park. My legs feel heavy, but I push through. Keeping my eyes peeled for this creature, I scan the area as I go. I don't know if it'll be here, but I have to try, so I head back to the spot I saw it in. The spot I stopped and talked to it. It clung to the shadows, but it came out enough for me to see it last time, maybe it will again.

"Come out!" I call, and hold my breath as I wait. A breeze blows by, a soft fluttering sounds behind me, and I look over my shoulder.

Caution tape.

There are still pieces of it up, some of it ripped down. The merry-go-round is covered in flowers, stuffed animals, and photos. I swallow past the sudden lump in my throat. How am I just noticing this all now?

I don't have much time. Someone could be patrolling the area. They'll want to know what I'm doing here. I can just tell them I wanted to visit the memorial, but they'd likely make me leave. I came here for answers, and I plan to get them.

I close my eyes, take another breath, and turn around.

There he is.

Chapter Twelve

VESPERON

I felt her before I saw her.

But then I saw her and all the breath left me. My body went still, and a calmness I have never felt before washed over me.

She is here.

And she is here for me.

We stare at each other for a long time. Seconds. Minutes. Hours. I do not know. I feel every emotion swirling inside her. Fear is at the forefront tonight, but lingering in the background is sadness, anger, hurt, betrayal.

Who hurt you, my love?

"Why are you afraid?" I ask, taking a small step forward.

"I'm not," she says, raising her chin.

I smirk. "There is no point in lying, little human. I feel your fear. Taste it on my tongue."

She purses her lips. Then takes a breath. "Okay. I'm afraid because... because I don't want to die."

"Why would you fear that?" I step closer. She does not move.

"Because of what you did."

"But I did that for you, little human."

"What?" she breathes out, her perfect eyebrows knitting together. Those perfect full lips turning down in a frown.

I step forward into the moonlight. My energy wanes as I become *less*. I lift my hand up, and through it, I see the moon. I smile, dropping my hand and meeting Lexia's gaze.

"Your eyes..." she whispers, hers widening slightly.

"They reflect in the moonlight," I answer. "The only thing about me that is not transparent." I squeeze my hand into a fist.

She glances up at the moon, then back to me. Awe still written on her face.

"They were saying terrible things about you. Those boys were making plans to sleep with you. Making bets. Saying dirty things about you. I could not let them do that."

"You... They..." A sharp breath leaves her, and her hand goes to her chest. "They were?"

"Yes, my love. They were not nice boys."

She frowns. "Why did you call me that?"

I take another step closer. Her scent permeates the air—vanilla and cinnamon—and I close my eyes to breathe it in. I expect her to move away from me, but she does not. When I open my eyes, she is still in the same place. Merely feet from me.

"Because you are," I whisper. "You have taken up every second of my thoughts since I saw you last. You said you were going to come back, but you did not."

Her face is unreadable, but I feel her confusion. It is at the forefront now, the fear almost gone. She glances over her shoulder, staring at the spot I killed that boy. The spot the other one should have died too. She looks back at me.

"You killed them—"

"Yes—"

"—for me?"

Closing the distance between us, I stop only inches from her and look down, wishing I could touch her, feel her soft skin. But I am not solid in this realm, and only ever would be if there were a bond between us. If that bond were completed, connecting me to her, then I would be my solid form. But until then, touching her will be nothing more than a craving.

"I would do anything for you, my love."

I stare into her bright-blue eyes, the light from the moon glistening off them.

"What are you?" she asks, reaching her hand forward but pausing before she touches me.

"I am a shadow."

"What does that mean?"

"Just as it sounds. I am a shadow as you know it, only I am a being."

She drops her hand, but I wish she had not. I wish she would try to touch me. Explore my being in every form.

"And what are you doing here?"

"Protecting your realm." Her eyes widen, and she glances past me. I try to hide my smirk when she looks back at me. "Perhaps I should add that I protect your realm from the darklings."

"Darklings?"

"The demons, the boogeymen, the things that go bump in the night."

"But you..."

"Do not usually do such things," I state, looking over her head at the spot those boys were. "I told you why I did that. I had to. I have never done anything like that before."

"How do I know I can believe you?"

"Because you have my heart." I press my hand to my chest, wishing it could be hers. It goes through me, because I am not tangible even to myself. It is a strange feeling, even after these thousands of years of it happening.

"Will you hurt anyone else?" she asks, tilting her head to the side.

My brave girl... All her fear is gone. Now, there is only curiosity.

"I will hurt anyone who threatens you without hesitation. Shadows are loyal and trustworthy. We take our purpose seriously."

"You said your purpose was to protect my realm."

"That is my duty. My purpose is to protect, cherish, and love my mate."

She sucks in a breath. I reach forward and run my fingers gently across her cheek. Her eyes fall closed, and her beautiful lips part. Lips I wish I could kiss with my own. "You are a masterpiece," I whisper. "I wish I could kiss you."

"Why can't you?" she asks, her lashes fluttering as her eyes open. I run my hand along her skin, not feeling it and hating that I cannot.

"Because you do not love me in return." I drop my hand, and she opens her eyes. I smile. "Perhaps one day."

We stare at each other, and I wait for her to agree. To tell me that one day she will love me in return. To assure me that I have something to look forward to. She does not, though. She pulls her gaze away and tugs out her phone from her back pocket.

"Shit," she hisses, then presses something on the phone and brings it to her ear. "Hi, Mom. No, I'm fine, I swear. Yeah, I'll be home in five minutes. Just... out for a walk." She sneaks a look at me. "I know that, but I'm fine. I just needed some air. Okay. Yes, five minutes. Love you." She shoves the phone back into her pocket, then looks at me with disappointment in her eyes.

"I have to go."

I nod and step back. "Return to me."

"I... will."

And then she leaves.

CHAPTER THIRTEEN

LEXIA

I have no idea what's come over me.

As I walk back to the house, I feel... good. There is something alluring about knowing that creature killed someone because they said something bad about me. Am I glad Jordan is dead? No, of course not. He was young and it's sad. Teenage boys say stupid things all the time, that doesn't mean he deserved to die. But knowing someone did something so severe in my honor is... It's hard to explain. It's hard to even comprehend because I know it's wrong. It's so wrong, but it's so romantic, in a dark and twisted sort of way.

My whole life, I've had no one on my side. Only my mother, but that doesn't count, does it? She kind of has to. She's my mom. Most parents are born with the need to protect their child.

This shadow person, he *chose* to do this. Something inside of him wants to protect me, for no reason other than he's compelled to.

He said he loves me.

Could that be true?

Is that... weird?

By human standards, yes. It's weird *and* creepy. But he's not from this world. And that's an entirely different problem.

How are there other worlds? Or *realms*, as he called them. If that's true, what else is out there?

Maybe my wish to be taken by aliens isn't so farfetched after all.

And what am I going to tell Bradyn? Oh my stars, he will lose his head if he finds any of this out. I can't tell him. He'd think I'm crazy. Bradyn used to be the only person on my side who would stick up for me, but... it was never by much. Mostly, people just left me alone because I was with him. He never actually told them to stop.

I look over my shoulder many times but don't see that shadow person following me. Does he have a name? Why isn't he following me? Can he? Do I want him to? What if I woke up in the middle of the night and saw him lingering in the corner? That would be scary... right? Yeah, definitely scary.

Yet, something about him makes me feel safe. It's the strangest thing and totally messed up. There's obviously something wrong with my head if I think I am safe with a shadow monster who admitted he killed someone who said something bad about me. That's a little dramatic.

But if he killed *for* me, it's unlikely he will kill *me*. So, I am safe with him, aren't I?

Until he turns on me, that is.

But would he do that?

What the hell has my life become? In a few short days, my prom is ruined, I find out my boyfriend cheated on me, my friend is dead, and now a shadow monster is in love with me.

He is *in love* with me.

At least, that's what he said. He could be lying. He could be saying all this to lure me closer to him so he can kill me too. How do I know he won't kill me? How do I know anyone won't kill me? Is he more likely to kill me because he's from another world? Or more likely to kill me because he's killed before? What the hell are the statistics on that?

Wow, chill out with the nerdy stuff, Lex. You're being nuts again.

Right. Tame down the nerd.

My mother is standing on the porch when I reach the house. She's frowning. I offer her a smile, but she doesn't return it.

"I'm sorry, Mom."

"Lex, come on. After what happened today?" She throws her hands up, giving me that disappointed-mom look.

"I know, but... I just—that's why I had to go. I needed to walk."

"Well, you could have at least gone the other way." She gestures toward the road away from the park.

"And told me where you were going." I give her an apologetic smile and she pulls me in for a hug. "I was worried. After your father, I just—" She sighs. "Next time, please just tell me where you're going."

"I will. Promise." I hug her back.

"Come on, let's go to bed." We head inside, and Mom locks the door. "Do you want tea or anything?" she asks.

"No thanks. Just going to bed."

She nods. "I'm working in the morning."

I give her another hug, then head to bed. She stays in the kitchen, and I hear her opening and closing cabinets. She'll have a cup of sleepy time tea and go back to bed. There's no school tomorrow because of what happened, so I'm not worried about being tired in the morning.

I change into my pajamas, but I don't go to sleep. Instead, I grab my laptop from my desk, hop into bed and turn it on. The rose gold MacBook was a gift from my mother for Christmas last year, and it's come in handy many times. I know she couldn't really afford it, but I needed a new laptop desperately. The one I had wouldn't hold a charge and only worked when plugged in. Plus, it was missing a few keys on the keyboard, and I'd get a black screen at least once a week.

I get comfortable, resting my back against the headboard, open the browser and search up content on shadow monsters.

A lot of what I find is fandom stuff. Characters related to video games or comic books. I also see a few ads for monster romance books which... seem interesting, but I ignore them for now. No one is talking about romance over here, I just want to know what this thing is and if I should be worried about it.

I dig through a few pages before I find a question someone asked on a forum that catches my attention.

I've fallen in love with a shadow monster; is that so wrong?

I stare at it for a long time. I've never heard of this forum before, and I don't know if it's fictional or someone being serious, so I click on it. I won't know unless I check it.

The page loads, and the question is in bright-blue lettering on a black background at the top of the page. Below it, in smaller white font, is information to the reader's question. I click on the "see more" button, then read.

When I was a child, I saw a shadow man standing outside my window. I told my parents, and of course they didn't believe me. It never felt evil or wrong. It just stood there and watched. My parents' idea of fixing it was to buy me better curtains for my window, but I always knew when he was there. I felt him. Even as a young child, I just knew. For years, this creature stood at my window and watched me. The moment I knew he was there, a comfort washed over me, and I was able to sleep soundly. Knowing he was watching over me made me feel safer than I ever had before.

My father was abusive, toward my mother and eventually me. Home wasn't good. But Nyhlym always made sure I was safe. Eventually, I talked to him, though he didn't speak back right away. I didn't understand why, until one day he did. He explained that he was far from his zone and in the moonlight, so it drained his energy, and that if I wanted to learn anything about him, I would have to meet him at his zone.

So, I did what any other eleven-year-old would do, and I snuck out the next night to meet him exactly where he told me.

This one-night thing turned into an every-night thing, because once I talked to him that first time, it became an addiction.

If I thought I felt good with him watching me, I felt even better talking to him. When he had more energy, it made me feel even better.

Of course, as I child, I didn't quite understand all of this, I just knew that I felt safe with him.

That first night, he explained that I was his mate. That the bond was so strong, he felt it already, even though I wouldn't yet because I was too young. Until I felt it too, he would watch over me and protect me, as that is what his purpose was. As a shadow person, he protects.

This went on for years.

Until one day, I felt it too.

I was eighteen. I snuck out of the house to meet him as I normally did, and when I saw him, I stopped dead in my tracks.

I felt it.

At that point, I knew everything he'd been telling me was the truth. That we were mates and destined to be together. There was no way I would ever be able to be without him again.

But how? We live in different realms, and he'd already explained that humans can't go to his realm, and the only way he can live here is if we complete *the mate bond . . . but we can't do that without him being solid, which only happens in his own realm.*

But once we could complete the bond, his connection to me would be enough that he could take on a solid form at all times—the way he is when he is in his own realm. See, when the shadow men are here, it takes a lot of energy and they are nothing more than shadows. We pass through them all the time and don't know because they can make themselves blend with the shadows, essentially invisible. They linger around, watching and protecting. Doing their duty of protecting us.

It's been seven years now since we've been together. Seven years that we've figured out a way to make this work, and we think we're closer to finding a safe realm for us to live, as the human world isn't good for him, and the shadow realm is impossible for me.

Though I love him with every part of me and know that we are meant to be together, I can't help but be hesitant. Once I cross over into another realm, I may never get back. It's a big decision, and I'm not sure what to do.

Which is why I am posting here and hoping for advice. I love this shadow man. He is my entire world and I've never felt so good . . . but I'm scared.

My heart is pounding as I finish reading the article. I scroll to the top to check the date. It was posted a little over a year ago. I scroll down to the comments and see only five. Three are along the lines of asking if she needs help or Jesus. Another is telling her good luck, but the final comment says that if that shadow man is her mate, then she should go for it. The commenter regrets missing her opportunity to do the same with her shadow man when he came to her in the night.

That's two people talking about this like it's real. Like it's a possibility.

I look toward my window—would I know if he were out there, watching me? Would I feel him?

I'm not in love with this thing and I don't feel any connection to him, but I can't deny that not being scared is something. And now that I know he is a protector, I guess safe is a simple way to describe my feelings.

I read through everything again, not sure if I should believe this. It could be a joke. Is it possible that other people have dealt with similar things, or is it all a hoax?

All I know is it feels real—and that's what scares me.

A short time later, I put my computer away and slide under the blankets to go to sleep. I dream of the school. Of walking into the gymnasium prepared for the prom, my dress perfect with not a single stain on it. The gym doors open on their own...

The room is dark, just one dim light shining from above, the stage barely seen in the background through the darkness. But standing there, in the center of the room, beneath the light, is my shadow. Tall, lean, confident. He turns to me, and though I can barely see his face, I feel his smile. He offers out his hand.

I smile, ducking my head. Then I lift my skirt and walk to him. I reach for him but hesitate. Will he be real? I look up at him slowly. He nods, one small tip of his head, and I know. I just know.

I take his hand, and it's real. It's soft yet firm. Oh my stars, it's perfect.

He pulls me to him, my chest pressing against his. His heartbeat is steady, chest rhythmically pulling in breaths.

"Beautiful..." he whispers, his voice a zephyr in the air.

He raises my hand, his other going around my waist. I place mine on his shoulder. Soft music starts in the background, and I recognize it instantly. It's one of my favorites.

"Dancing on my Own" by Calum Scott—I always preferred his version.

My shadow moves, and I move with him. Gracefully. Perfectly in sync, like I was made to do this. Like we were made to do this *together.*

As the song plays and we dance this beautiful dance, I grow confused. The lyrics of the song make no sense to how I'm feeling. Not when it comes to him... so why this song? Then I remember the pain I felt of seeing Bradyn with Cassie.

But that's far from my mind.

All there is now, is me and my shadow.

Just us. The way it was supposed to be from the beginning.

CHAPTER FOURTEEN

VESPERON

My feet move without me realizing, and before I know it, I am feet from her house.

She turns down a small walkway and meets another woman standing on the porch. They share words I cannot hear from here, hug and go inside.

I blink a few times and look around. I am away from my zone. I do not believe this area is overlooked by a shadow, but I know it is not mine to watch over. Mine spreads across the park and the school, not among the homes. When creatures cross over, it is through the darkness, not out in the open like this, as there is not enough space for them to squeeze through. We need ample space to move through realms.

I glance toward the park. It is quiet. Calm.

Being gone for a few more moments will be fine, I think.

I move through the lawns, sticking close to the houses and cars so I blend in if someone is looking outside. I move through bushes and fences as if they are not there, until I am at her house. Lexia's house. I peek through the windows, seeing through the sheer curtains, and spot her mother and her sharing more words. They are blurry through the fabric, but I would know my Lexia anywhere. When my love moves down a hallway, I move with her, glancing into every window. The next two I pass have thick blinds and curtains. I cannot see through them, so I keep going. I move around the house, and find a room with the light on, the curtains parted just enough for me to see inside.

Mint-green walls, a bright-blue comforter on the bed, a small desk, and then...

The air leaves my lungs when I see her.

Lexia's smooth, creamy skin on full display. What I would give to run my hands over her curves. Her hips are full, her legs thick. I want to touch them, feel their warmth and softness. I would kiss every inch of her for hours, days, years, if she would let me.

I watch, mouth agape, as she changes her clothing, the need to be with her almost too much to ignore. I cannot break into her house. I could, it would be so easy to walk in, but that could cause more problems than I need. It is bad enough I am breaking all these rules for her now.

I should not be here.

She picks up a device from the desk, then sits in her bed. She opens it, and I recognize it as a laptop. I stand there and watch her for so long, each second harder than the next. All I want to do is be with her. It is only when a car blasting music drives by my laser-focused attention is broken and realize I need to get back to my zone before something happens.

"Soon, my love," I whisper, stepping back. "Soon enough, we will be together."

"Jlenar requests your presence immediately."

I glance toward my door and find a guard I do not recognize standing just inside my room. With a sigh, I follow him through the halls to Jlenar's office. This guard does not seem to be watching me more than any other would, so I cannot imagine Jlenar thinks I am responsible. Though, if he is calling me into his office again, he must know something. I am not sure what happens to those who do what I did. It is clear I will be stripped of my title, the duty of guardian no longer mine. But what then? I will be kicked out of the castle, that is certain. Will I be given another duty? Brought to the prisons? It would be an opportunity to escape. To go to the human world, get Lexia, and find somewhere safe for both of us.

I keep my back straight and my head high as we walk. *I am innocent. I am innocent. I am innocent.*

I repeat the words over and over in my head, hoping I believe them enough to get through another meeting. Maybe Jlenar knows nothing—doubtful but possible.

When we reach his office, the guard knocks, then announces, "Vesperon, sir."

Jlenar gestures with two fingers for me to come in, then points to the chair in front of his desk as he sits in his tall one.

I walk past the guard and sit down.

I am innocent. I am innocent. I am innocent.

"I need you to give me every detail you remember about this man who was walking the dog on the night those teenagers were attacked."

I try not to act shocked by his request, and instead nod. "Anything to help, sir."

"Are you talented with drawing?" he asks, tapping his finger on his desk.

"I am."

He pushes a notepad and pencil toward me.

"Take as much time as you need."

I scoot the chair forward and pick up the pencil. I push the sharp tip to the paper, but look up before I begin. "May I ask why?"

The shadow of his lips forms a thin line. He folds his hands together and places them in front of him. "There has been another attack, only two towns over. They are different, but similar enough that authorities are considering they could be done by the same person."

Gods be damned...

My eyes widen, and Jlenar huffs. "I've spoken with the guardian on duty there, and they said they also recall seeing a man, though there was no dog. Can you... draw the dog as well?"

"Of course, sir. Anything that will help."

As I work on the sketch of the man I know is innocent, I make sure his features are prominent, this way he cannot be mistaken as the person responsible for this new attack. Unless, in some crazy twist of events, he is the one responsible. What are the odds?

I make his hair dark and messy, his nose long, and his eyes happy. The man always seems happy, though he is out because he cannot sleep. Once I am finished, I flip the paper over.

"Do you have another pencil?" I ask.

Once I have a new one that is sharpened, I draw the dog. It is a large dog, though I am not sure on the breed. It is fluffy and its fur is three colors—white, grey, and black. It is also a happy dog, very energetic. It enjoys playing fetch with sticks that have fallen to the ground. When it is cold, it wears a matching jacket with the owner. I do not think this man is capable of hurting someone, but you never know. I have no shame letting an innocent man take the fall for this if it means keeping me with my mate.

It does not take me long to finish the dog, and when I flip it back to the drawing of the man, I slide the notepad toward Jlenar. He picks it up and looks it over.

"This is very helpful. Thank you, Vesperon." He flips the page, looking over the dog and nodding. Then he puts the pad down, gets to his feet, and holds out his hand. "Keep up the good work."

As I grasp his hand, I swallow hard.

Why have I been put in such a terrible predicament? Choosing between my mate and my duty. I look into the shadowed eyes of Jlenar and wonder if I should tell him. Perhaps admitting that the spells did not work and I feel my mate would be for the best. Maybe the Shadow Chief would make an exception and allow me to do both, or they might relieve me of my duty and allow me to be with my mate, or maybe... maybe they will redo the spell, and this wonderful feeling I have will go away.

No, I cannot risk it. This feeling, I never want it to go away. I would rather them strip my guardianship than take her from me, and something tells me that is precisely what they would do. They consider me theirs, their property. I work for them. Why would they let me walk free for love? They would not. Not for love. Not for anything.

I give the chief a small smile, and say, "Anything to find the being responsible."

CHAPTER FIFTEEN

LEXIA

School drags. People ignore me all day, which I am thankful for, though I do feel bad because it's due to them being upset over what happened to Jordan and Scott.

Sadness settles over the school like a blanket, and no matter where I go, it's there. Suffocating. Choking. I've run to the bathroom three times so far to splash cold water on my face, and I kind of wish they'd go back to picking on me instead of this.

Knowing this is all because of me—*for* me, it's hard to process.

As I walk the halls, I listen to the conversations. I have no one who will tell me what's going on, so the only info I get is what I hear in passing. It's not much.

Jordan's services will be tomorrow evening, the funeral the following day. Scott still hasn't woken up, and doctors aren't sure if he will. If he does wake, they aren't sure what state he will be in as he had a lot of damage to his head.

I haven't heard from Bradyn, even though he said he would call me. I haven't seen him either. Late afternoon, I find out he and the rest of the team skipped today and are having their own memorial for Jordan.

I think of texting him, but I shouldn't. I don't want to give him the wrong idea.

Maybe today is the day I should talk to my mom about what's going on with Bradyn and me, this way she can help me figure out how to handle this.

Dealing with being angry with him while wanting to be there for him over losing one of his best friends isn't easy. It would not be easy for anyone, never mind a clueless teenager like myself.

When I get home, Mom isn't here yet. I didn't expect her to be. When she works first shift, she gets home closer to four. I bring in the mail and look through the envelopes, noting there is a one from the state addressed to my mother. I know what it is before I open it. With shaking fingers, I tear it open and have to read through the letter four times before I know what it says.

Dear Lydia Keissenger,

This letter is to inform you that Ted Yelle has been approved for release on June 24.

We have no information on his address. You will be notified of this information as soon as possible. If you have any questions, please reach out to Landon County Jail.

I grip the paper in my hand so tight it crumples. Tears sting my eyes. How the hell is he getting out so soon after what he did? It's been only eight years. The guy deserves life. I take a few steadying breaths, fold the paper, and put it back in the envelope, then hide it under some clothes in my closet. My mother doesn't need to see this. She doesn't need something to be stressed out about. Ted doesn't know where we live, and he shouldn't be able to find out. Why would he, anyway? I'm not a kid anymore, and apparently, that's what he's into.

I do homework while I wait for Mom to get home. I get through all my math and the first draft of a chemistry paper before the front door opens and Mom announces her arrival. I close my computer and head into the kitchen.

"Hey, Mom."

She smiles at me as she puts a few grocery bags onto the counter.

"Hey, sweetie. How was school?"

"Kind of rough. Everyone was upset."

She looks at me over her shoulder with a frown.

"I'm sorry, Lex. It'll take time, but everything will settle."

I shrug. "Graduation is coming up. Not sure it'll be better by then."

"You'd be surprised how quickly things change in high school."

She's not wrong. I can't even keep track of half the stuff the students are up in arms about. It changes like the weather.

"Do you have a lot to do tonight?" I ask.

She looks at me with a raised brow. "Just cooking dinner, why?"

"I was hoping we could talk."

She turns, pressing her back against the counter. "About?"

I rock back on my heels, clasping my hands behind my back.

"Bradyn and I kind of broke up."

Her eyes widen before her hand comes up to cover her mouth. "Oh, Lex..."

She pulls me into a hug.

"It's okay, Mom. Really, I just—I'm trying to figure some stuff out." She nods against my shoulder, squeezes me once more, then lets me go.

"Talk after dinner?" I nod. She smooths my hair down, then goes back to pulling the groceries out of the bag. I go back to my room to finish my homework.

Dinner is delicious, as it normally is. Mom is a great cook. She went to college for culinary but then ended up pregnant with me. Her and dad talked about opening a restaurant when I was older, but then... well, she didn't want to do it without him. It was their dream.

"So, what do you want to talk about?" Mom asks as she clears the table.

I pick up my water, wondering if this was a good idea. What if one day I forgive Bradyn and want to be with him again? Will Mom forgive what he did? I don't want to lie to her. I plan to tell her the whole truth, but I don't want her to hold it against him forever.

"Before I tell you, you have to promise to give me neutral advice, and not look at this like a mom." She pauses as she reaches for the dish of rice still on the table and pins me with a glare. "Mom," I warn.

"Fine, as long as it isn't something bad."

"It's bad, but not *really* bad. I mean it is, but it isn't like he hit me or anything like that."

She nods, then goes to the sink.

I finish my water and bring her the glass. I hop up on the counter and watch as she washes the dishes. After a moment, I blurt it out.

"Bradyn and I broke up because he was cheating on me."

"He *what*?" she barks, turning toward me. The dish that was in her hand drops to the sink with a loud clank, causing water to splash on the counter. I flinch away.

"Mom," I groan, resting my head back against the cabinet. "Just let me finish."

"Fine," she relents, and goes back to washing the plates. I can sense her tension though, as if she's worried I will ask her how to get even with the girl or how to make him want me back. She's scrubbing that plate like it's the one who cheated on me.

"I know it sucks, trust me. I'm upset about it. I'm hurt and embarrassed. We've talked a few times. He said he knows he messed up, but I'm not ready to forgive him. I don't know if I ever will be."

"I'm proud of you for that."

"Thanks, but that's part of the problem."

"How so?"

"Jordan was one of his best friends. Bradyn is really upset. I want to be there for him, but I'm worried he's going to get the wrong idea, and I don't know how to... do this. How to balance it, you know?"

Mom nods as she washes the last fork, then shuts off the water and turns as she wipes her hands on the dish towel.

"So you're worried about setting boundaries because you don't want to hurt him because he's already hurting?"

"Pretty much, yeah," I say with a sigh.

Mom steps up to me and smiles, then cups my cheek. "How did I raise such a smart girl?"

I smile. "Good genes."

She chuckles and sucks in a deep breath.

"Relationships are never easy, but stuff like this is hard, Lex. The only thing I can say is to be honest. Let him know you are still upset with him but want to be his friend right now because of what he's going through. That you'll be there for him in a platonic way, but nothing more. If he can't accept that and pushes those boundaries, then you need to put your foot down and remember that's the choice *he* made. Putting space between you and him would be due to what he's done. It's his choice. Don't feel bad for protecting yourself."

"I just don't think he's thinking clearly right now."

And that's the problem. He's not in his right mind.

"And that's probably true, so it's possible he won't respect your boundaries. You may have to put your foot down and tell him you need space, but that doesn't mean it'll be forever. Maybe one day he'll realize he messed up this situation too, or maybe one day you'll want to reach out and see how he's doing again, and that's okay too."

I hop off the counter and hug her.

"Thanks, Mom."

"Anytime, sweetie."

I head to my room and do more homework until my mother falls asleep. Then I sneak out of the house again, needing to see my shadow man.

CHAPTER SIXTEEN

VESPERON

She comes to me early tonight, much earlier than last time, and I could not be happier.

"My love," I greet her the moment she is close enough to hear me. I step from the shadows and walk to her, my body vibrating with energy. I feel it growing stronger, feel her affection toward me. Her curiosity. The fear is not here now, but there is still sadness lingering. A deep-seated hurt that has been there since that first night, before I killed that boy for saying bad things about her. She carries sadness around with her, and it calls to me.

She smiles when I reach her, and I smile back.

"I wish I could hold you," I tell her.

"You can't?"

I shake my head. "Not properly. Hold up your hand." She does. I press mine against hers, and it goes right through. Her eyes widen, and she darts her gaze to me, as if she doesn't remember the last time I touched her. Maybe she didn't quite understand then.

"Will you always be like this?" she asks.

I shake my head again. "One day, perhaps, I will take on a solid form."

"When?"

"Soon, I hope."

She chews on the inside of her lip, then looks over her shoulder. "Can we sit?"

"You can, if you'd like. I would fall through."

She looks down at my feet. "But you don't fall through the ground?"

"Nature is magic. I can use natural things like the ground and trees, but anything else I go right through."

"Do you need to stay in the shadows?"

"It is preferred but not necessary."

She looks around, still biting her lip as she scans the area. "There is a fallen tree, just beyond the slide over there."

How thoughtful my mate is...

"Then that is where we shall go."

I let her lead me there, though I know the spot she speaks of well. I remember the night this tree fell. It was during a storm with heavy winds and rain about ten years ago.

She sits on the tree, and I lean against one in front of her. She is such a beauty. Exquisite. A sight to behold. A precious treasure.

"I appreciate your thoughtfulness," I comment.

She smiles at me, and I want to melt. She is breathtaking.

"What is your name?" she asks, tilting her head to the side.

"My name is Vesperon, but you may call me Ves."

Her lips turn up into a soft smile. "That's an interesting name."

"Much different from the human names."

"How do you know so much about humans?" she asks.

"I have been around for a very long time, my love."

"How long?"

"Thousands of years. Though, I have only been here for about five hundred."

"Wow..." she breathes out as she looks around. "That's... you must have seen so much."

"I have. It is amazing."

"I bet." She goes back to chewing on her lip, looking down at her feet. She is unsure about something. "Can I ask you something?"

"Anything."

"Are you... Am I your, uh... mate?"

Hearing the word leave her lips has my body flooding with warmth. I recall hinting toward her being my mate. I made a comment, but again... perhaps she didn't catch on. She was too worried about other things to fully grasp what I was saying. I will forgive her for this because she came back to me.

"You are," I admit to her, hoping it will not make her run.

"How do you know?"

"I can feel it." I press my hand against my chest. "Right here. I felt it from the first moment I saw you, and it never goes away."

"Why don't I feel it?"

"It is different with humans, I hear. It takes longer sometimes." She nods, then looks out toward the park. "May I ask you something now?"

"Sure." She blinks, looking toward me.

"Why are you so sad?"

Her brow furrows. "I'm not."

"I sense it in you. It is what drew me to you that first night. I felt your sadness when you entered my space, and when I saw you, I felt the mate bond. But your sadness... it has been with you ever since that night."

"You can sense my sadness?"

I nod. "All of your emotions. They call to me."

She shakes her head. "That's weird."

"I think it is wonderful. It makes me feel good."

She smiles. "I guess it isn't so bad, then, but really, I'm not sad. I'm just... confused."

Though she says she is not sad, I know she is. It is there, rooted in her. Perhaps she has dealt with it for so long that she ignores it now? Maybe it has become a part of her. I choose not to push this because I do not want her upset. She may be in denial about it, or just does not want to talk about it right now. Though I wish my mate would talk to me about everything and anything, I know I must give her time and space.

"I sense that too. Your confusion is strong toward me."

"I don't understand how any of this is possible."

"I understand."

"I mean, monsters are real? Shadow men are real? What else?"

"Everything," I say with a shrug. "Anything you can think of. The fairy tales and stories are all real, based on different major events through time. The monsters are less likely to come into your realm now that the guardians have taken over, but they still do."

"You weren't always guarding us?"

"There were always guardians, but not as many and not as organized as we are now. We have a new king in our realm and he has done great things for us and protecting everyone."

"Why do you do it?"

"Why do we protect?" She nods. "It is who we are. It is what we do. Not all of us are born with that instinct though. There are plenty of shadows who are bad. We protect you from them too. But we are born to be protectors. It is what our purpose is."

"So you all just linger in the shadows and protect my world?"

I gesture around us with a slow wave of my hand. "Many worlds. All over. Not only here."

"That's hard to wrap my head around."

Silence falls over us for a few long moments. I cannot pull my gaze from her as she stares up at the sky with wonder and intrigue in her eyes. The stars are bright tonight, twinkling.

"Are you sad because I hurt your friend?" I ask.

She turns her head toward me. "I'm sad he is dead because he was young. I like to think he would have grown up and not been such an idiot, but now no one will ever know. Mostly, I'm sad about it because another friend is really upset about it."

"I am not sorry for what I did," I say adamantly.

She winces, then nods. "I don't want you to be," she whispers. Then she huffs out a laugh and shakes her head, staring down at the ground. "It's... hard to explain, but it feels good knowing that someone protected me for once."

Her voice is so quiet, I hardly hear it over the rustling leaves.

"No one has done that before?"

She shrugs. "Not really, no. I've always kind of fended for myself."

"What about your parents?"

"My father died when I was little. My mother does her best."

"Friends?"

"I don't have many. In fact, I don't really have any at all. One, maybe, but probably not for much longer."

"Why is that?"

"Because he betrayed me."

"You should not be with people who hurt you," I say, stepping closer to her. "You should be with people who want you happy, who make you happy. Be with people who make you feel good. Who love you for who you are and nothing less."

She looks up at me, her blue eyes bright through the darkness.

"Is that you?" she whispers.

"That is me, my love. I swear to you, I would never do anything to hurt you. Never." I run my fingers along her skin, barely feeling it but even the slightest tingle helps ease my ache for her. Her eyes fall closed, and gods, what I would give to kiss her. To make her mine.

Her eyes open, and then she says something that shocks me.

"If I asked you to kill someone for me, would you?"

I do not have to think before answering.

"In a heartbeat."

CHAPTER SEVENTEEN

LEXIA

"Miss Keissenger?"

I look up from the paper I'm doodling on to see Mr. Nomi staring at me over his rimless glasses. He's one of those people that looks grumpy all the time. No matter what. Even if he's happy about something, he looks mad. So I can never tell how upset he really is.

"I'm sorry?" I answer innocently.

"The homework, Miss Keissenger. Number eighteen, please." He huffs.

"Oh, right. Uh..." I flip the page back to the one I did my homework on, then scan the page until

I find number eighteen. "Y equals two. X equals seven-point-three."

"That's correct," he grumbles, moving his gaze to the student behind me. "Number nineteen, Miss Leile."

I turn the page back to my doodle and smile to myself when I see what I was drawing. I hadn't even realized what I was doing, but the image has my chest fluttering. My drawing comfortably leans toward Chibi style. A lot of people think it's stupid and childlike, and maybe it is, but it's adorably fitting. My shadow man looks especially cute short and stubby, standing next to me, looking down at me with hearts in his eyes. I'm blushing but looking up at him with just as much emotion. What is it about him drawing me in? Could it be possible that we really are mates? That I am like those girls on the internet who are mated to a shadow man? I don't feel it—when will I feel it? The only person I can ask is him. *Ves.*

I laid in bed for an hour last night, thinking about what he said.

He'd kill someone for me in a heartbeat.

Having Ted killed would be one less thing my mother would need to worry about. She already does so much in taking care of us. She's worked her ass off for years to make sure the bills are paid, and I have everything I need. She won't allow me to get a job because she wants me to focus on school. Aside from that, him dead will save someone else from what I went through. No one deserves that. No one. I know he'll do it again. A man like him, a predator of the worst kind, they don't change. They don't stop. They are who they are, and nothing will make them change. He'll go after another young girl. Another innocent, unsuspecting victim, and I can't allow that to happen.

I need Ves's help.

Mom is working the overnight shift tonight, so I won't have to hurry back. I can stay with Ves all night if I want to.

I stopped by Jordan's services to pay my respects to his family. The funeral is tomorrow morning, but I won't be going, so I wanted to make sure I at least stopped by today. I went first thing, and I'm grateful there weren't too many people there.

When I get home, I eat quickly, and change into something more comfortable before hurrying to the park.

Ves is standing at the edge of the trees, waiting for me. Almost like he knew. Maybe he saw me or sensed me, but he knew.

He smirks when he sees me, and I walk to him. Every ounce of fear I once had over him is gone. There is nothing for me to fear about this shadow man. I know that. Somehow, I know he won't hurt me. That everything he has said about protecting me is true. I look at him and feel safe. I stand in front of him and feel protected. Like I'm in a bubble and nothing could penetrate it because he won't allow it.

"You are happy today," he says with a smile that makes him look less intimidating. To me, anyway. To everyone else, he likely still looks like a monster. But the more I spend time with him, the more I see how animated his face actually is.

"I'm excited to see you."

"That elates me, my love." I smile a big bright smile that hurts my face. It falls when I remember what I wanted to ask him. "What is wrong?" he asks, stepping forward. He raises his hand to my cheek, like he always does. It tingles, feeling like nothing more than a warm brush of air.

"You feel like..." I whisper, closing my eyes. "Like a warm breeze."

"Is that bad?" he whispers back.

I open my eyes and see he looks almost sad.

"I only wish I could really feel you."

"One day."

In the darkness by the trees, he is all shadow. But I've noticed when he steps into the moonlight, his eyes glow dimly, almost like a reflection. The full moon is gone, though, and the nights are darker than usual.

"When I accept that you are my mate?" I ask.

He drops his hand. "It is not only about accepting, it is about the universe allowing you to feel it. I will become whole when we complete the mate bond."

"I want to feel it. All of it."

"We do not have to wait for it..." he says, stepping forward.

My heart does a little flutter. "Wh-what do you mean?"

His hand brushes along my arm, the feeling like the softest blanket. Then it moves around my waist, and his ghost of a touch, though barely there, is comforting.

"I ache for you," he says in a low tone. "I think of you every time I get into bed, wishing I could touch you and taste you." My lips part, and I let out a breath. Is he talking... *sexually*? "You have consumed me, my love. Your face is the first thing I see when I wake, and the last when I go to sleep."

"But how can we..."

"I have heard of things, of spells." He steps back and shakes his head. "I do not know if they will work, and I am not sure how to find them, but it is worth a try. I am desperate for you. I need you."

This shadow man, this creature, literally takes my breath away with the things he says. Is it possible to make this sort of thing up? I can't imagine saying these things if he didn't mean it...

"There is a spell to make you real?" I tilt my head to the side, his words finally sinking in. I was so caught up in his words and how he sounds, that I missed what he actually said.

"I am real," he mutters.

"To make you... able to touch me?"

He nods, then steps back into the shadows. "I am stronger here, in the dark, but it is not enough. There is light all around us, even if you can hardly see it. Mating with you would make me take a solid form here, but if we can find a spell, then we will not have to wait."

"Where do I look?" I ask, stepping toward him. I recall from the forum the issue the girl had. He cannot take a solid shape here. She cannot go to his realm. So how did they mate? What does mating entail?

"I do not know. There are people in my realm who may know, but it is too dangerous to look for those sorts of people. If my chief finds out, I will be in trouble, and I am unsure what will happen to me."

"I have an idea," I say.

"What is it?"

"I don't want to say just yet. In case it doesn't work, but I'll start looking as soon as possible."

"Each day gets harder and harder to ignore this feeling. I am afraid by the time I am able to touch you, I will never want to stop."

I roll my lips between my teeth, ducking my head. "That's okay," I say when I get the confidence to look at him.

"Is it, my love?" he teases, stepping forward. "You will let me touch you as long as I want?" My mouth goes dry as I nod. "All night? All morning?" I nod again. "Forever?" he rasps, reaching for me again.

"Yes."

He hums out a satisfied sound, then looks up at the sky. "This feeling is... overwhelming. I am afraid I am going to lose control and do something that will get me into trouble."

"Please don't do that."

He looks back at me.

"I cannot stand not being able to have you," he says.

I'm beginning to feel the same way...

"It won't be long," I say. "We will figure this out."

He lets out a sigh, and nods. "Will you tell me what is wrong now?" I tilt my head to the side. Nothing is wrong. Everything seems so perfect in this moment. "Before, your face changed and I felt it. Hesitance? Worry?"

"Oh... that." I clear my throat, then move closer to him, press my back to the tree and slide to the ground. "Last night, I asked if you would do something for me..."

"Are you referring to asking if I would kill someone for you?" He takes a seat beside me, resting his hands and feet flat on the ground. I nod but can't meet his eyes. "You only need to tell me who, my love."

"I don't want you to get into trouble."

"I will not."

"You are able to travel where you want?"

He shakes his head, his gaze out at the park. "Not exactly, but it matters not." He turns to me, his face so dark I can hardly make out the features. "Did this man hurt you?"

"Yes."

"Then there is no question. Give me a name, and I will find him."

"He's still in jail. He's..." I wet my lips, then rest my head back. "He's getting out soon. A little over a week."

"I will take care of it," he says. "Give me a name."

"Ted Yelle," I answer. "He's at Landon County Jail." Ves nods.

"I need you to do me another favor," I say.

"Anything, my love."

"Promise me that you will not harm anyone unless I say so."

I see his brow furrow from the corner of my eye. "I do not understand."

I'm terrified he will somehow find out about what Bradyn did to me and kill him. I may be angry with him, but I don't want him to die.

"There are some people in my life who have hurt me, but I've decided to forgive them." True for some, not for Bradyn, but I still don't want him dead. "I don't want them hurt."

"But I cannot promise to only kill those who you give approval of. What if you are in the middle of being attacked?"

That is a valid point.

"Okay, then unless I give you approval or my life is in imminent danger."

He thinks this over for a moment, then nods. "I will agree, but I do not like it."

"I appreciate it more than you know." I put my hand over his, staring at how his blankets mine like a black cloud.

"You will have to show me how much you appreciate it when you can feel me," he rasps. I blink up at him.

He's definitely making sexual comments now... right?

"H-how?" I ask.

"By pleasuring me with that beautiful mouth of yours."

My heart skips a beat. Oh my stars, that's the hottest thing someone has ever said to me. Who knew words could make my stomach flip like that?

I blink again, and my gaze goes between his legs.

"Do not worry, my love, there is a cock there. It is just hidden."

Holy hell, did he just say the C-word?

"Hidden?" I question, because the shock of that is more than what he said.

Ves gets to his feet and moves to stand in front of me. He looks so tall from down here. He steps back so I can see him better. The bit of light shining behind him makes him look so interesting. I can see right through him, but because of that, I see his features much clearer. He is like the most beautiful charcoal drawing. Everything is shades of grey and black. He is muscled, toned in all the right places, tall. And his face... strong jaw, full lips, and eyes that look like they've seen horrible, horrible things.

"As a shadow person, I am amorphic, meaning I can take on any shape I want. We prefer the shape of man because it comes naturally to us. We have the body parts we need to use for walking and picking things up. We can speak and see and do everything we need." He crouches down in front of me. "Besides, I would not be able to speak with you if you were so distracted by my leaking cock at your presence."

"Holy shit..." I whisper under my breath. I lick my lips and try to hide the fact I'm panting.

He smirks again, then looks down my body and back up to my eyes.

"I could have two, if you wanted."

"Two c-co—"

"Cocks." He huffs out a laugh. That's the first time he's laughed. My embarrassment makes him laugh? My innocence? "Yes, my love. Two. Any size. As thick as you want them. As long as you want them. Any shape too. If you want it smooth, it will be smooth. If you want it ribbed, then it will be ribbed. I will give it to you any way you would like. The only thing you have to be prepared for is my cum." He smiles a devious smile as he takes me in again, his heated gaze looking me up and down. I feel frozen, unable to move. I'm so turned on, my pussy grows slick. "Us shadow men cum a lot. Much more than humans do, but the best thing is... it tastes good." The last few words come out in a husky whisper, and my stars... How is this turning me on so much?

107

"You know what it tastes like?" Why that's what I ask, I have no idea.

"Mm, I do. It is common for shadow men to be with other shadow men. It is our only means of pleasure. We have needs and are not allowed to be with the women."

"Why not?"

I can't say that I'm mad about it. I feel possessive over this monster, and I don't want to think about him with any other woman, human or not.

"Because our duty is to guard, not to reproduce. That is for others." He leans in, closes his eyes, and inhales. "I can smell you. Feel your need for me," he says through gritted teeth. He opens his eyes, and somehow, I see the need in them. "You are going to make me lose my mind. I need to touch you," he growls. His breathing grows heavy, his chest heaving the same way mine is. "I have an idea. Do not move." He stands and heads toward the playground.

I don't move an inch.

CHAPTER EIGHTEEN

VESPERON

I may literally explode if I do not get a taste of her soon. I have never in my existence been so needy for something, never needed to come so badly, but it must wait. There is nothing I can do about it now. But for her... there is something I can do.

She is struggling as I am, but she is not used to having to hold in those feelings. I will show my mate just how giving I can be. Let her have a taste of what is to come when we can finally be together.

I walk across the playground, to the spot near the trees where there are clusters of wildflowers and pick a large blanket flower I have seen growing for quite some time. It is the most vibrant shade of orange and red, and now, it will be my tool.

I do not know why, even in less than solid form, I can touch anything that is natural—the dirt, trees, flowers—but tonight, I am grateful for it. Grateful for whatever magic nature holds that allows me to utilize it.

I walk back to my mate who is sitting in the same spot. She did not move, exactly as I said.

"I need you to get up and remove your pants," I tell her.

"What?" she breathes out.

"You are not leaving this park until I make you come. Now get up and remove your pants."

I do not miss the surprise in her eyes. It is humorous. If I were not so on edge, I would laugh. She gets to her feet but looks around.

Is she worried about being caught? Perhaps.

I would not be happy if someone stumbled upon us and saw her naked. Especially if it was that man with the dog...

I jerk my head toward the woods, and she moves deeper inside. Following after her, I grasp onto the flower like it is my lifeline.

"Stop," I say, once we are deep enough. She stops, then turns toward me. Her chest rises and falls quickly, and though I would love to see every inch of her, that will wait until I can touch her, appreciate her beauty. "Pants off," I demand. She reaches for the button of her jeans, flicks it open, pushes the zipper down and shimmies out of them. "Lay them on the ground and sit on them so you do not get that delicious ass of yours dirty."

She does exactly as I say, and I am so thankful for such a well-behaved mate. I am told these humans tend to be stubborn. Mine is perfect. The hesitance in her eyes only makes me want to do this more. She is unsure about this but is listening to me anyway. Does that mean she trusts me? Of course she trusts me. She asked me to kill someone for her. She is here and comes every night now.

Her caution is tinged with fear, and it floats around her like a soft cloud. It is not too thick, just enough to make me smile.

"What are you afraid of?" I whisper, dragging the flower up her calf.

She whimpers, her eyes falling shut.

"I don't know," she mutters.

"Being caught?" I ask.

"I think so."

I drag the flower past her knee and along the inside of her thigh. She trembles and I smile.

"No one will see us in here. Lie back and let me make you come." She nods, and lies back. "Will you be a good girl and do as I say?" I ask.

"Y-yes."

"Move your panties aside," I tell her, knowing I am unable to.

With shaking fingers, she does as I say.

"Gods be damned, if that is not the best thing I have ever smelled." I lean down and inhale her sweet scent, my mouth watering. Tasting her would be a dream. One day, I will get a taste, and I will never stop. I stay there for a moment, close my eyes, and just breathe. I need to keep it together. Her scent is intoxicating, the sight of her dripping for me is... gods, I am going to lose my mind. I sit back but keep my eyes on her sweet cunt.

"Spread yourself open," I say through gritted teeth.

"Wh-what?"

"You are dripping wet, aching to be touched. These beautiful pussy lips are not allowing me to get to your needy little clit."

Her eyes are as wide as saucers, but she says nothing. She does as I said, though, and uses both hands to spread herself. From here, I see how tight she is. I am aching to stuff her with my cock, allowing me to make it as big as possible so I can feel her tightly wrapped around me, stretching her as much as she can take.

"Has anyone been inside you before?" I ask, holding my breath as I await the answer.

"Y-yes."

He is now on my list of victims. Anyone who touches her, or who has touched her, will die.

Then I remember the promise I made her and grit my teeth.

Damn it.

"How many?" I ask.

"Ju-just one."

Well, that is not so bad. Still, he will have to die.

I drag the flower along her calf again, and her body trembles. I run it along the crease of her thigh, then over her stomach and down the other side. Her body moves into the flower, wanting more, and I wish I could give it to her.

"Patience, my love," I whisper.

This will have to do.

Holding the stem between my thumb and first two fingers, I bring the petals toward her clit. I turn it sideways, then roll it so the petals swipe her clit one at a time.

She moans, her hips rolling against the flower.

I smile as she chases the pleasure.

Rolling the stem the opposite way, she moans again. Her pussy clenches, causing it to drip. I wish I could lick it up. I pull the flower away and drag it along her thigh again.

My love whimpers, and I chuckle.

"What is wrong?" I ask.

"I'm already so close, and... and..."

"And you do not want me to stop?"

"No," she answers.

I smile to myself. "Tell me, Lexia, how will you have me when we mate?"

"Wh-what?" she says, her voice straining as I run the petals up her thigh.

"One cock or two?"

"One," she says.

"How thick?"

"I don't know."

"As much as you can take?"

"Yes!" she cries out when I drag the petal along her clit again.

"You will let me breed you," I say, spinning the flower along her clit again.

"Anything you want..."

"Anything?"

"Yes!"

"Such a good girl," I say, then lean close to her pussy, still spinning the flower back and forth. I have no idea if this will work but I try it because my mate is right there. So damn close.

I take in a breath, then blow it out slowly.

She cries out, her body jerking in front of me, her pussy spasming hard. When I am whole, she will be tied down so she cannot move away from me, so I can watch her pussy contract and drip. She will come and come and come until her body is too weak to fight. And then I will make her come again.

Oh, the gods have blessed me with such a perfect mate.

CHAPTER NINETEEN

LEXIA

I can't believe I let a shadow man, a creature from another realm, give me an orgasm! And with a flower! A flower! Something that is so delicate and beautiful and... we defiled it!

Oh my stars, and what did he do with it? What if someone finds it? What if a child picks it up to play with it? I'm a terrible human! How could I do such a thing? I'm so embarrassed.

My legs are jelly as I make my way home. I don't want to leave but I have to. Ves's eyes are on me until I turn the corner, and I don't stop and look at him like I want to because if I do, I won't leave. I need to get home to bed to sleep. It's bad enough I fell asleep after Ves made me come like that. What if I hadn't woken up, and Mom got home to find me gone again?

How the hell did he make me come like that?

All he had was the dainty little flower. He didn't even have his hands, yet... my entire body felt like it went through some kind of amazing explosion—like a volcano. Bradyn and I had sex a few times, and he made me come often with his mouth and hands, but not like Ves did. Never like that.

I smile to myself until I get home, then stop in front of my steps when I see someone sitting on the porch. They're leaning against my door, legs pulled up, hands on their knees, and head buried.

I glance at the sneakers—Bradyn.

Why is he here?

"Bradyn?" I hiss. He doesn't stir, so I move closer and call his name again.

This time he lifts his head and wipes his face. "Hey," he says, giving me a tired smile.

"What are you doing?"

He gets up, yawns, and stretches. "Waiting for you."

"Why?"

"Because I wanted to see you." He looks around. "But it seems you were hanging out with someone else."

I can't tell if that was meant to be a dig or not.

"I wasn't with anyone." I cross my arms over my chest.

"No? So you hang out with yourself until"—he checks his watch—"two a.m.?"

Two a.m.? Damn, that's late. This is the longest amount of time I've ever spent with Ves. And it wasn't enough.

"What do you want, Bradyn? Why are you sleeping on my porch?"

He looks out at the street. "I just needed to see you."

I sigh, and move up the steps to unlock the door and go inside.

"How did you know my mom wasn't home?"

"My mom told me. I guess they ran into each other at the gas station earlier."

"Well, you shouldn't be here," I say as I lock the door. I turn, and he's there. His arms are on my waist and he's pulling me against him, burying his nose in my neck.

"I miss you, Lex."

"Bradyn..." I try to move, but he won't allow me to. "Bradyn, please stop," I whisper.

"I can't. I missed you. I'm so sorry for what I did. I need you to forgive me."

"I can't."

"Yes, you can. I need you to. *Please.*"

"No, Bradyn. It's not that simple."

I push against him again, and this time he lets me go. I step back, putting plenty of space between us.

"Lex—"

"No, Bradyn," I say, my voice shaking. "I don't know what you're thinking, but if you're using Jordan's death as an excuse to act like this, it's not okay. I can be your friend, because I know you need that after what happened to Jordan and Scott, but that's it. You hurt me. You hurt me so bad, Bradyn. You betrayed me. I can't forgive you for that, and if you can't accept it, then don't bother talking to me at all."

By the time I'm done, tears are pouring down my cheeks. The lump in my throat is making it hard to breathe, but I focus on taking slow, steady breaths.

117

Bradyn is just staring at me. His eyes slightly wide, lips parted. He blinks a few times, then runs a hand through his hair.

"You're right. I'm sorry, I just don't know what to do," he mutters. "I feel so lost. I fucked everything up, and I don't know how to fix it."

"You can't fix it, Bradyn. You can't fix any of this. What's done is done. You need to figure out how to deal with it and move on."

He nods, and pulls out the chair from the kitchen table and sits. He drops his head, and I give him a minute before I speak again.

"I want to be your friend, Bradyn."

"I know, Lex. I just don't know how to only be your friend."

I want to say he should have thought about that before he messed around with Cassie, but I don't because it's just mean.

"It's not easy for me either," I say, then move toward him and sit in the other chair. "We can figure it out together, but there needs to be boundaries."

"I understand..."

"Like no more sleeping on my porch or sneaking through my window." He nods. It's silent for a few moments, so I get up to get us each a bottle of water. I place his on the table and take a sip of my own. "Are you going to the funeral in the morning?" I ask.

"Yeah, the whole team is going."

"Then you should go home and get some sleep," I say.

He looks up at me, his eyes red. Then he glances at the couch. I huff out a sigh.

"I swear, Bradyn, if you try coming into my room, I—"

118

"I won't. I swear, Lex. I just don't want to be alone."

I get to my feet, nodding. "You'll have to be gone by six so my mom doesn't catch you."

"I will, I promise." He gets to his feet and opens his arms for a hug. "Friends?" He smirks. I shake my head but lean into him and give him a hug.

All I can think about is how it doesn't feel right. How I wish this were Ves.

Chapter Twenty

VESPERON

After placing the flower between pages 612 and 613 of my Guardian Handbook, I carefully close it. I stick it on the bookshelf, beside the other four books I own, and stare at the spine for a long time, recalling the events of last night—a memory I will never forget. Not the way she sounded, the way she moved, the way she smelled, the way she looked—and gods, I can hardly wait to experience the way she tastes.

A knock on the door has me turning. I expect to see Jhai, but when I see Jlenar, I pause.

He does not look happy. His lips are in a firm line and he is glaring. He is in my room. The chief is in my room.

This is not good.

"We need to talk, Vesperon." His tone is deep, serious. He does not wait for a response. He walks in and shuts the door behind him. "You know why I'm here, do you not?"

"I am sorry, sir, but no. I am not sure why you are here."

"There was a report made. A complaint of you interacting with a human."

My body goes ice cold.

They found out.

How the hell did they find out?

I do not respond, just continue to stare.

"Your lack of response leads me to believe this is not a false accusation."

"It is not," I admit through a rush of air.

"May I ask why you would go against your oath as a guardian?" He is stiff, both in the way he is standing and the way he is speaking. I feel his disappointment. Shadows only feel the emotions of other shadows when they are strong. When I first became a guardian, Jlenar said he saw immense potential in me. He felt I was a strong-minded shadow and would do well. No doubt he is second-guessing that today.

I grit my teeth, knowing only the truth will help now. There is no excuse they would ever accept, but perhaps the mate bond will make this easier.

"She is my mate."

"Your mate?" he barks. He runs a hand over his head, then chuckles. "Impossible. You can do better than that, Vesperon."

"It is the truth, sir. I assure you, the girl is my mate. Nothing else in this realm or another would cause me to be unfaithful to my duty."

He looks me over, and I expect him to shout at me. To scream. Or to sentence me to death or something just as crazy. But he nods. "You enjoy your work as a guardian?"

"Of course, sir."

"Then you will meet with the Shadow Witch tonight before your shift. She will complete the spell again. This way we will not have to worry about mates."

My fingers twitch to strangle him. He will not take this feeling away from me. He will not take Lexia away from me. But how can I argue? I told him I enjoy my duty as a guardian. What will happen if I argue? Had I said I wanted to be with my mate, what would happen then?

"Sir—"

"And if you choose to not go, Vesperon, I will make sure this mate of yours suffers so badly, that you, too, will wish you were dead. Do I make myself clear?"

I lift my head, gritting my teeth. There is no doubt in my mind he feels the rage coursing through me, the same way I feel his disappointment.

"Yes, sir," I choke out. I have no other choice but to accept. Not if I want my Lexia to be safe.

There is another knock on the door, then it is pushed open. This time, it is Jhai. He has a smile on his face, until his gaze moves to Jlenar. Then his eyes widen, and the smile falls.

"Good day, Vesperon," Jlenar says, turning on his heel and moving past Jhaixl without acknowledgment.

Jhai stares at Jlenar's retreating form for a long moment, no doubt as shocked as I was to see him. The chief does not visit us in our rooms. Jhai looks back at me, then closes the door.

"What the hell was that about?" he asks.

I wish to tell him the truth, but he will not understand. Guardians will never understand such a thing because we all took the oath to not have mates. No one will understand this unless they have felt it, and I am in no mood to explain to him why this is so important. What am I to do? If I meet with the witch, she will take away what I feel for Lexia. If I do not meet with the witch, there is no doubt in my mind Jlenar will harm Lexia. Shadow men are great assassins. It is what makes us excellent guardians. I am stuck.

"Ves?" I shake out of it and blink a few times, meeting Jhai's concerned gaze. He gestures behind him. "What was that about?" he asks again.

"He came to tell me that the sketch I drew was helpful in finding the man who killed that boy."

Jhai's eyes widen. "He came all the way here for that?" The hesitance is evident in his tone. He does not believe me. I do not blame him. I would not believe that story either.

I shrug. "He was extremely grateful, I suppose. You are as surprised as I was."

He stares at me for a moment, then nods. He takes a seat on my bed. "I thought you'd be sleeping."

"Then why come in?"

He smirks. "You know why."

I smirk back, but his once appealing self is no longer alluring. The way he touched me was always good, but now, all I want to touch is my Lexia, and I do not want

123

anyone else to touch me either. Everything that I am is for her and her only.

"Another time, Jhai. I am sorry, but I am tired."

He nods. "Understandable." He gets moves to the door. "You know where to find me if you change your mind. Sleep well."

I wave him off, then get into bed, but I cannot sleep. All I can think about is what I am going to do about the Shadow Witch.

After tossing and turning for hours, barely getting any sleep, I crawl out of bed. I sit on the edge, scrubbing my hands down my face and wishing I knew of a way to fix this. I should have been more careful. I should have known they would be watching me after what happened. Hell, I did know that. But, for some reason, I had not thought they would be watching me up there. Only assumed it would be here, on my way, which now that I think about it, makes absolutely no sense. I was careless and it will cost me.

I stand and stretch. There is a knock on my door. I do not think it has been used so many times in one day before.

"Come in!" I call out when the person on the other side does not enter, which only confuses me as to who it could be. The door opens upon my words, and I find a guard on the other side.

"I am here to accompany you to see the Shadow Witch. Are you ready?"

So Jlenar does not trust me to go on my own? Interesting. Better than death, I suppose. But why are they allowing me to live? They have killed for less. There is no wasted time here. If you mess up, you are done. Why do I get another chance? Perhaps I think too harshly of them and killing is not done so simply.

Or perhaps it is because this is a mate thing and not fully my fault? Perhaps it is the Shadow Witch who will pay for this? I never asked for this. In fact, I took an oath to give up my mate. I cannot help it did not work and I found her. I cannot be blamed for poor magic.

I grit my teeth but nod. "I am."

"After you," he says.

I step into the hallway, and he closes my door. His heavy footsteps sound after me as we walk down the hall, down the stairs, and outside. There are shadows walking all around. Some coming and going from shifts, some gatekeepers, some guarding this castle.

The Shadow Witch's grounds are in the opposite direction of my zone, and a twenty-minute walk, which is not much compared to some places. There are areas in our realm with cities and transportation vehicles, like the human world, but the guardians have no such things. We have the absolute minimum. They do not want anything to distract us. We are stripped of everything, keeping only what we need to survive and complete our duty appropriately.

When we reach the rusted iron gate, we stop and the guard presses the button on the brick wall to alert her of our presence. I look around, noting how much these grounds look like a place the humans would enjoy on the holiday Halloween. The trees are all bare of leaves, the brick wall is crumbling, and the hut itself is set up on a small hill, a silhouette to the dark-blue sky.

"Who's there?" a voice calls back from the intercom on the wall. It is a man, not the Shadow Witch.

"Quetz. I'm here for the witch."

"Witch is not in."

The guard looks at me over his shoulder, then glances back at the wall.

"Jlenar spoke with her himself," he grunts.

"She had an emergency. She'll be back in an hour if you want to wait."

"My shift is in an hour," I say.

The guard huffs, then goes back to the intercom. "Call her back sooner."

"No can do."

The guard turns to me and points a finger. "You will go to your shift, and you will not act up. I am unaware of what is going on here, but Jlenar is away for the evening, so I have no choice but to make this decision. When your shift is done, you will meet me here, do you understand?"

I nod. "Yes, of course."

At least this gives me time to talk to Lexia.

Or better... make a plan of escape.

CHAPTER TWENTY-ONE

LEXIA

"What's wrong with you tonight?" I ask.

"Hm?" He looks over at me, a blank stare on his face.

I roll onto my side. "You are not speaking as much as you normally do."

"I am just tired. I did not sleep well."

"You sleep?" I ask, and he laughs, though it is not full of humor. It sounds almost forced.

"Yes, I sleep. I have a mind that needs resting, just as yours." His tone is clipped. He is frustrated tonight and I only wish he would tell me why.

"Can't you sleep now?"

He shakes his head. "I could, but that would be dangerous. If anything were to happen, I need to be alert."

"How is being half asleep being alert?"

"You are a smart girl." I smirk at him, and roll onto my back. "Tell me about your family," he says.

Mom is working another third shift tonight, and I've already been here for an hour, just talking. Ves has asked me lots of questions, and he's just been sitting there, listening. Getting to know me better.

"My mother is the best. She's always done everything she can to make my life good, even though hers hasn't been."

"Why do you say that?"

"My father died—he killed himself when I was only six. I don't remember much. I... was the one who found him." I go quiet for a moment because this is usually the point when I get pity. The point when people give me the "Oh no, that's so terrible" and "That must be so hard. Are you okay?" but Ves doesn't. He does none of that, so I keep going. "I don't remember finding him, only that my mother told me I did. Anyway, they were really in love. Really happy. They were each other's soulmates, and ever since he died, Mom hasn't been the same. She doesn't smile the same. I see the photos of her and my dad together, of all of us, and her smile now... it's just sad. Especially after the stuff with Ted."

"Tell me about that."

I've never talked about it before. I went to a counselor for a year after it happened, but she felt I was dealing with it okay, and so we stopped. Talking about it only makes people weird around me and so I choose not to.

"My mother was dating him. He was the one and only man she dated after my father, and I'm certain she'll never date someone again because of it. They were together about a year, and he started—" I sigh and close my eyes. "He started touching me about six months after they were together."

"Go on."

There is this darkness to his voice, this rage I know is because he is angry for me. I don't usually talk about this, but I want him to know what that man did to me, because then he might make sure he gets what he deserves. I can't believe I am thinking that way, but that man ruined my mother's life and made mine horrible for a long time. He deserves nothing but pain.

"Before it got physical, I'd wake up and find him in my room. Just standing over my bed, looking down at me. I'd ask him what he was doing, and he'd say he was checking on me. Then I'd wake up to him sitting in my rocking chair, just watching. He'd tell me everything was okay and to go back to sleep. He did this for a while, and eventually, I'd wake up and he'd have his shirt off. Then his pants. Then... he was completely naked. I will never forget the night I woke up to see him... touching himself," I whisper the last words, fighting away the nausea. I can still picture it, which I hate. If there was anything I could erase from my brain, that would be it.

A soft sensation flows over my hand, and I look down to see Ves's shadow hand covering mine—through mine. I look up at him and he nods, telling me to keep going. So I do.

"I didn't know what to do, so I pretended I didn't see him and went back to sleep. I didn't understand why he was touching himself; I was only ten. That happened quite a few more times before he was standing over my bed and doing it. Then I woke up to him making me touch it. He would make a show of how good it felt, then told me he could make me feel good too. But when he touched me, it never did. Of course I was just a kid, so why would it? It was always wrong and gross—"

"This man deserves the deepest parts of hell."

"Yes, he does."

"He will get that when he dies."

"How do you know? Have you been to hell?"

Wow, Lex, did you just ask him if he's been to hell?

"I have not, but I have heard about it. All the guards in this area share a castle, and that castle is not too far from the prison. I have spoken to many throughout the years who have worked there and helped out in hell, so I have heard countless stories."

"Who chooses where they go? The bad people?"

"The universe. There is magic and energy all around us. Watching and keeping track of what you have done in this life to make sure when you move on you go where you belong."

"Will you go to hell for what you've done?" I question, looking up at him.

"No, my love. I will be with you always."

"Why?"

"Because you are my heart, and I plan to keep that with me forever."

He smiles down at me, and I smile back. His words always have my chest fluttering.

I say, "I mean, why won't you go to hell."

"Ah... well, not all creatures are susceptible to that sort of judgment. Because of my duty, I am exempt from certain things. Since a lot of shadows are meant to kill to protect, it does not count against us."

"Then how do they stop people from killing everyone?"

"By having guards like me to stop them."

He smiles, then leans back against the tree.

"I wish I could feel you," I whisper, looking up at him as his eyes fall closed.

"Me too, love. More than anything."

CHAPTER TWENTY-TWO

VESPERON

Lexia leaves deep into the night, and I am left with the worry of what to do. We had an amazing night together, and so many times I wanted to tell her it would be our last. But I could not bear the pain I would see on her face.

I am thankful she cannot feel the bond yet, and perhaps it will not be so bad for her. Perhaps I will not remember what it feels like to love someone. That is hard to believe. This feeling has consumed me, how will I not remember? Maybe the witch can cleanse my brain and make me forget all of it. She is a witch, after all. She has magic. But that also means she has magic to do other things too.

Like make Lexia fall in love with me. Like make me whole so we can mate. Mating here is impossible due to my not being solid, and she is unable to travel through the shadows to where I am solid. Our mating seems like an impossibility, but it cannot be. Why would the universe choose us for one another if it were?

Do I risk asking the witch to do such a thing, or do I allow her to put this spell on me and forget Lexia forever?

There is only one answer, only one right thing to do.

When my shift is done, I head to the witch's grounds as Quetz told me to do. It is the only thing that will keep Lexia safe. I cannot risk her life. If this Shadow Witch reports me for trying to coax her into breaking the law, Lexia and I are both done for.

"Almost didn't expect you to show," Quetz says as I reach the gates.

"I am not one to break rules."

He looks at me as if he knows that is a lie, but he said himself he is unaware of why I am here. It is doubtful he knows anything and is just being rude.

"Let's go. She's waiting."

We walk through the open gates, up the dirt path, then up the steps to the porch. There are a mix of dried herbs and crystals hanging from the rafters on the porch from frayed string. It looks as it did the last time I was here, all those hundreds of years ago. Quetz knocks on the door. Though, this witch is a different one. They are only human and have a normal human lifespan.

A moment later, the door is opened by the witch, who looks entirely human. She is not a shadow person, but an actual witch who was blessed with shadow powers, which is why she is here with us. She is one of the reasons our world needs artificial lighting. She looks at me, her eyes flashing with excitement, then she steps aside. Quetz moves to walk in, but she holds her hand up. Keeping her eyes on me, she says, "Not you."

"Excuse me?" Quetz snaps.

She pulls her gaze from me and puts it on him. "My appointment is with him, not you."

"I am here to escort him."

"And you have done so. Now, I will take over. You can take a seat on the porch and wait until we are done."

"But—"

"I can get in touch with Jlenar if there is a problem?" she warns, raising a brow.

Quetz growls but moves away from the door. He pins me with a glare, and I look back at the witch. She then smiles at me, and I walk in. He grumbles something under his breath, but I cannot make out what it is.

The moment the door is closed, she speaks in a hushed voice. "You are fascinating."

I furrow my brow and turn to her. "Excuse me?"

"It has been hundreds of years since this has happened."

This... I can only assume she means the spell not working.

"This has happened before?"

She nods. "Every now and then, there is a bond so powerful that even magic cannot stop it." I raise a brow at her. "Though, there is the chance that the spell just didn't take right the first time."

"How will we know?" I ask.

"Aren't you going to ask me to not do this?" she says instead, tilting her head to the side.

"I had considered it..."

"But?"

"I realized it was not worth the risk. I do not want any harm to come to my Lexia."

"So you'd give up what you are feeling—"

"To protect her."

She nods, then steps farther into the room, going down a short hallway. She gestures for me to follow her, so I do. We end up in a cramped room. The walls are lined with shelves full of jars and books and stones. In the center, is a dark-wood round table and two chairs. It is made of the same dark wood that Jlenar's desk is made of.

"Sit."

I do, and she takes the seat across from me.

"What is it you were going to ask me?" she says.

"Are you asking me this to report to Jlenar?"

"Never."

"Why?"

"My duty is to the realm, not just the guardians. If your mate bond is as powerful as I think, then there may be more to it than we understand."

"What does that mean?"

"I am not at liberty to say at this time. Not until we are sure."

"How can we be sure?"

She presses her hands flat to the table. "First, tell me what you were going to ask of me."

"I was going to ask for a spell to make me whole so we can mate in her realm, then to help us find a place we could be safe."

"Such as?"

"I do not know of one, which is why I was going to ask."

She nods. "There are many, just so you are aware, but I will not share them with you."

"Why not?"

"How will I know if this is because of a strong bond if I give you all the answers? True love must be put to the test. If it withstands everything, then it is true. It is stronger than anything else in this world."

"What is happening here, then?" I look around, growing more and more confused by the second. Is she not going to fix this? Will my feelings for Lexia not go away? Is she going to help us?

"I am going to put the spell on you again. You will forget your mate. I am unsure how long it will last. The strength of the bond will make that decision."

"If I am going to forget her, then how will I know to fight the bond?"

"If you are what I think you are, then you will remember her, and in remembering her, you will cause another spell I am going to put on you to go into effect. There is no need to fight anything. The universe will do what it is meant to."

This woman is confusing. Spell on top of spells?

"Another spell? For what?"

"You will be free."

"Free? How?"

"In the moment you remember her, it'll be like a wall has fallen down and memories of this morning will come back to you. You will know who she is, recall what you've done with her and for her. You will remember everything I am going to tell you. The wall will let loose this spell that will allow her into the realm, and for you to travel through the shadows with her and to another realm hidden beyond us. But before you travel, you must complete the bond to keep her safe. People will be looking for you, Vesperon. This will not be easy."

"Which realm?"

"You will have to find that out yourself. I cannot help you, but if you make it through, it will be worth the reward."

I frown, leaning back in my chair. "Why are you doing this?"

"Reasons I cannot say, but if I am right, and I usually am, then there are big changes coming." She pauses, looking at me with excitement in her eyes. "Are you ready, Vesperon?"

No, not really, but there is no other choice. What this woman is saying does not make sense, but the love I have for Lexia is strong, so perhaps it will make sense one day. But what does this witch mean that this is part of a bigger picture? What else could be going on here? I do not understand any of it. The only way I will know is if I come back from this spell. But what if I do not?

I have already accepted that part. I have accepted I will not remember Lexia, but as long as she is safe, then it will be okay.

"I am ready."

She turns her hands palms up and moves them closer to me. "Place your hands on mine. Close your eyes and listen to each word spoken."

I remember this from the last time. She speaks some ancient Shadow language that barely anyone knows anymore. I picture Lexia's face in my mind, the way her face lights up when she smiles, the way she looks when she is nervous... the way her body twitches when she comes. I think of all the nights I spent with her and hope they will not go away. I do not want to lose these memories. They are the best thing to ever happen to me.

"Emduh es enuh hah. Ewah hock pul jhu enuh wen jadi jeh ecks. Heh ket ler neh ewhem nesh. Eehu kawel enyed oelatch veed, Vesperon."

I blink, opening my eyes and feeling as if I just woke up from a deep sleep. The witch is in front of me, and for a moment, I am confused. I look around, trying to remember why I am here..

"Vesperon?" she calls. I bring my attention to her. "Do you know why you are here?"

I search my memory but cannot recall. I remember walking to the gate, walking up the path, meeting her at the door, then walking in here.

"I do not," I respond.

"There was a bit of an accident, and it caused part of the spell to wear off. I just had to tighten it up for you."

"Oh, okay. Thank you, Shadow Witch."

She smiles at me, though there is something nervous about the look in her eye. She nods and stands. "Your escort is waiting for you on the porch. He will take you to the castle to sleep before your next shift." I get up and look out the window to see the usual dark-blue sky. My head is pounding, but at least I can go to sleep before I have my shift.

"Is it normal for you to spell during the early morning?" I ask.

She chuckles as we walk to the front door.

"Never. But I had an emergency last night and made an exception for you. You're such a strong guardian, Jlenar didn't want to go even a night without you."

I smile proudly at her. "I appreciate that. Thank you for those kind words, and thank you for making an exception and helping out the realm."

She winks at me. "Anything for the realm, Vesperon."

CHAPTER TWENTY-THREE

LEXIA

I stay after school to use the library to do some research for my final English paper.

My final paper.

Until college, that is, because I do plan on attending. I just want to take a year off so Mom and I can do some things together before I leave. That's the plan. Has been for a long time.

The sky is growing dark by the time I leave, and I wonder if Ves is at the park yet. As I exit the trees, I notice the sun is still up and know he will not be there. He told me he does not come out until the sun is completely down. Mom is working the overnight again tonight, so I'll come back when she is gone. The same way I have been doing the past week. I used to hate when she worked third shift because I didn't like being in the house alone at night, but now I prefer her working this shift.

I pass the road that leads to the park and look down it with a smile.

"Soon, Ves," I whisper.

I wonder if he is thinking about me right now, the way I am of him.

He says he sleeps when he is not here, so maybe he's dreaming of me.

I can't wait for us to finally be able to be together.

I need to do more research tonight before I go see him. Each night I get closer and closer to finding something to help us, I can just feel it. If I could spend all day looking for a way for us to be together, I would, but unfortunately, I can't. Not with school, my mom lingering, and graduation right around the corner. Still, I think I have some good leads. I went back to the forum and branched out from there. I dug around and found the email address of the original poster and sent an email, but if she is no longer living in this realm, she probably can't check her emails.

After passing the street, I round the curve of the road and notice flashing blue and red lights. I move my feet quicker and stop dead in my tracks when I see police cars and an ambulance in front of my house.

My house...

My feet move faster than they ever have. My door is wide open, and a police officer is walking out. The same one who was at my house the night Jordan died.

"Mom!" I shout, running up the walkway. I step onto the first step, but the officer grabs me around the waist.

"You don't want to go in there, darling."

"Where is my mother!" I shout. "Let me go!" I try to break free and get into the house, but his grip tightens on me.

"Come on, we're going to talk," he says, guiding me away from the house. I fight him, but he doesn't let me go. "Come on, darling."

"Where is my mother!" I scream. I feel the eyes of the other officers on me, but I don't care. I want to know where my mother is.

"I'm gonna tell you, but you need to come with me."

The promise of him telling me where she is has me cooperating. We move to the side of the house where there is a bench. My heart is pounding so hard, I'm going to throw up.

"Go on. Sit down," he says, then kneels in front of me. "When was the last time you saw your mama?" he asks.

"Uhm..." I run my hand through my hair and look around. "Yesterday. Last night before she went to work."

"Not this morning?"

I shake my head. "She got home after I left for school. She had to stop at the grocery store."

He frowns, nodding.

And it's then I know.

I just know.

"What..." I start, but I can't finish.

"Darling, something bad has happened. I'm real sorry to have to tell you this, but your mama is gone."

Gone?

"No—"

She can't be gone. She's probably just at work.

"I'm sorry."

"She... she can't be gone. She probably just stayed at work late. She just—Wh—How?"

He takes in a deep breath, then gets to his feet and sits beside me.

"Someone hurt her real bad."

I narrow my eyes and look at him, confused. Hurt her? How? Who? My gaze goes to where the park is. My heart sinks in my chest.

Was it Ves? No. No way. He wouldn't do that. He loves me. He wouldn't hurt someone I love. He promised to not even hurt anyone who hurt me, not without my say so.

"Is this—"

"Nothing to do with the incident at the park," he says, almost like he knows. How does he know?

"She's gone?" I whisper.

"I'm afraid so."

My eyes blur with tears, and then I lose it. The officer pulls me to him, rubbing my back, whispering he's sorry and he'll do what he can to help. We stay like that for a long time, until I finally settle. I feel like there's an elephant on my chest, but eventually the tears stop coming, and I can breathe a little easier. My whole body is numb though.

"What happened?" I finally ask. I barely feel a thing but I want to know what happened. How could all these bad things be happening in this area? How is my mom gone?

He sighs. "It's not good."

"I need to know," I growl.

He nods. "No matter what, you have to promise me you won't ever think this is your fault, okay?"

My fault? Why would I think this is my fault? My first thought is that it was Bradyn, pissed because I wouldn't go back out with him. He isn't capable of something like this, is he?

"O-okay," I say carefully, that elephant sitting down on my chest again.

"You know a man named Ted Yelle?"

The world around me stops. Everything just stops. I stop breathing, stop thinking. For a moment, I wonder if I died too.

But then I snap out of it. Shaking my head, I say, "He's in jail."

"He was released."

I shake my head. "No, the paper we got in the mail said he was getting out on the 24th of June."

He narrows his eyes, then looks beyond me. "Hey, Charlie!"

I look over my shoulder to see another officer pop his head around the side of the house. This one is much younger.

"Yeah?"

"Get me that report, please."

A moment later, the man comes over and hands Deputy Charmaine a paper. The young one gives me an apologetic smile.

"Thanks, Charlie. We're good here."

Charlie nods, then heads back to the front of the house.

Deputy Charmaine looks over the paper he was given.

"You're sure the letter said the twenty-fourth?"

I nod. "Definitely. I've been counting down the days to..." I can't finish what I'm going to say.

He sighs again. "He was released on the fourteenth, darling. There must have been some kind of clerical error. Or a typo."

"So he's been out for—"

"Almost a week."

"He did this?" I whisper, looking at him with pleading eyes. "H-how do you know?"

"You're too young to be hearing this type of thing, in my opinion, but unfortunately, this is the world we live in," he says more to himself than anything. He shifts and rests his forearms on his knees. "He killed your mama, then killed himself. He left a note."

He killed my mother, then killed himself...

"Why... why would he do that?"

"He was angry. Said it was—well, he just couldn't take the blame for why he was in jail."

I'm going to be sick. I'm definitely going to be sick. This can't be happening.

I get to my feet, and I run.

"Hey, darling! Where you going?" the deputy calls. I don't answer, I don't stop, don't turn around.

All the way to the park, to talk to the only person I have left.

"Ves!" I shout as I run up the walkway. "Ves, where are you?" I call out.

I move up and down the pathway but don't see him. Is it too early? I look up in the sky. The sun is gone. The moon is out. He has to be here. I move into the woods, but I don't see him anywhere. I check everywhere I can, every spot we've been in together and every spot we haven't. I call his name, over and over and over.

I press my back to a tree, taking a moment to catch my breath. The lump in my throat is so big I can't breathe. I need to calm down.

Calm down, Lexia. Just calm down.

I push off the tree and move toward the pathway, and that's when I feel him. I whirl around, noting the area around me is dark and I can barely see a thing. I'm deep in the woods, deeper than I should be.

"Ves, is that you?" I ask.

"How do you know my name?"

"Wh-what? It's me, Lexia." I move closer to where his voice came from. "I really need you to come out and stop playing games, Ves. Something bad happened," I explain through sobs. Still, he doesn't show himself. I move through the trees and finally see a bit of light from the park so move that way. "Ves, please!"

My legs are trembling as I make my way to the edge, then glance back inside, hoping he will come out. Finally, he does, and... there's something different about him.

"Something happened!" I shout. "Something really bad, Ves. That man, the one I asked you to kill, he... he—"

"Who are you?" he asks. I snap my mouth shut, looking up at my shadow man through blurry eyes.

"What?" I choke out.

"How do you know my name?" he demands, stepping even closer.

For the first time since I've known him, he looks scary. Actually scary. Like a true monster.

"What's wrong with you?" I ask. "You told me your name!"

"I have never done any such thing," he spits. "You are human. I am not allowed to speak with you."

My eyes widen, and I take a step back. "Why are you doing this? Why are you acting like you don't know me?"

He moves closer to me, getting into more of the moonlight, and I see how angry his eyes are. "I have never seen you before. You are just a human. I suggest you take whatever witchcraft you have been playing around with and go somewhere else with it before I make you disappear myself."

I choke out a sob, stumbling back. My eyes stay on him, and all I see is anger. Disgust. I can't breathe. I can't fucking breathe!

"No..." I whisper, shaking my head. *No, no, no!*

I look around me, wondering what is happening. How is this possible? Frantic, I look back at Ves, ready to plead for him to stop playing games because this isn't funny. I need him, now more than ever.

But he's gone.

You can get the next book in the series here:

https://www.books2read.com/lightingtheway

Join my Mailing List!
Not only will you get four free stories, but you'll
get updates on my books, adorable puppy photos, a
hilarious meme, and book deals!

https://quelltfox.myflodesk.com/nlbooks

AUTHOR NOTES

I love this story so much. I think Ves is one of my most favorite characters. The RH does start to form in the next book, so don't worry! Lost of spicy stuff to come ← see what I did there?
Thank you for your support ♥

Follow me on your favorite platform...

FIND THEM <u>HERE!</u>

https://quelltfox.myflodesk.com/m53srspiuu

About Quell

Romance with a Bite of Magic

Quell, an individual enamored with various art forms like painting and crocheting, found a profound passion for writing that eclipsed all others. As a USA TODAY bestselling author, Quell has graced numerous book signings, delving into the enchanting realms of steamy paranormal romance, especially the allure of reverse harem tales.

Residing in Massachusetts, Quell navigates life's
adventures alongside a cherished family of five
children, a dog, and two cats. Rainstorms, fuzzy
blankets, and loud music are some of her favorite
things, and there is nothing more beautiful than a field
of sunflowers.
Nothing brings Quell more joy than receiving emails
from fans, discovering they were captivated by the
inability to tear themselves away from Quell's books.
The profound emotional connections to the characters
foster a bond that extends far beyond the pages penned
by Quell.
https://www.quelltfox.com

Made in the USA
Middletown, DE
23 August 2024

59056488R00092